Money, Masks & Madness

Jennifer Bogart

Money, Masks & Madness

Copyright 2013 by Jennifer Bogart
Cover design copyright 2018 by Joanne Kasunic
Author Photo by Geri Photography

Print ISBN: 978-0-9949593-0-0
Digital ISBN: 978-0-9949593-1-7

This book is a work of fiction. Names, characters, places and incidents are products of the author's imagination or are used fictitiously. Any resemblance to actual events or locales or persons, living or dead, is entirely coincidental. No zombies were harmed in the writing of this book.

All rights reserved.

No part of this book may be reproduced in any form or by any electronic or mechanical means including information storage and retrieval systems, without permission in writing from the author. Thank you for respecting the hard work of this author.

Acknowledgements

James, my husband, for taking care of the "real world" while I live in my head, introducing me to new experiences (which almost always find their way into my writing), and offering unending support in everything I do.

Sharon, your enthusiasm and support mean the world to me. Without your constant reminders, need for perfection, and mad-ninja editing skills, this book might never have been completed.

Joanne, for all your creative energy and patience.

I still (and will always) hold you responsible for this journey I've embarked on.

My Beta Readers: Melissa L., Susan, Jennifer B., Jennifer M., Mandy, Lorna, Clair, Marcy, Shelley, Melissa M., Olga and Lucy. You're a special group and I couldn't have polished the book without you.

Special thanks to all my wonderful friends and family who helped along the way with support, encouragement, and patience.

This book is dedicated to my parents.
I love you Mom and Dad.

Prologue

Once upon a time, when the world offered adventure, the sun twinkled hope, and the birds chirped excitement, Tulip entered the world. A scrawny baby: red, wrinkled, and bald. Her mother took one look at her and sighed in dismay; another girl to add to the collection. She had four already and she was running out of flower names.

"She's simply stunning," the midwife proclaimed with far too much excitement. She was bustling around the room, putting away this and that. "Look at her adorable little face, that button nose, those rosebud lips. She's another beautiful blossom to add to your collection."

In that moment, Jane was feeling more like a wicked stepmother than a loving mommy. It was true that she lived a fairy tale life. Their home was a modern log cabin in the woods, surrounded by Mother Nature's luscious beauty. They grew their own food, kept a couple of goats for milk and cheese, and let the chickens run wild. Although they had the basics of electricity and running water, their life was rustic, with no outside influences such as internet or television. Jack had a prosperous business growing and selling organic foods and medicinal herbs at a local market which allowed them to maintain their simple lifestyle.

The door squeaked open and a mop of frizzy hair peeked through the crack, followed by giggles and a matching set of blond curls.

"Can we see?" Iris asked. At seven, she was clearly turning into a little mother hen. Already she was adept at doing laundry, foraging for roots, mushrooms, and other edibles in the forest, and keeping track of her younger sisters. Of course, she would be the first to want to meet her new sibling.

"Why, of course you can. Bring your sisters!"

The midwife's enthusiasm was grating and started to dig a hole in Jane's heart. Since the matronly woman's role had been to help with the delivery, she had energy and eagerness to spare.

Jane motioned to her girls to enter the room. They did so as quietly as four young children could, smothering giggles, and jostling to be close.

"She's ugly." This came from Rose. Honest to the core, and with absolutely no filters, she called it like she saw it, even at the ripe old age of four.

Iris shushed her sister and moved closer for a better look. The baby was now swaddled tightly in a ratty old blanket that may have been pink at one time but had faded to a sickly grey. Shrugging, she turned away and picked up two year old Lily so she could have a better look.

Lily popped her thumb out of her mouth long enough to burp and promptly stuck it back in. Shuddering, Iris put her sister down before the drool could drip off Lily's chin and land on her arm. With nothing more to see, Lily scampered outside, no doubt to return to the mud pie she had been creating in the backyard.

Sweet natured Daisy approached the bed with caution. Gently she peeled back the blanket and took a long look at her baby sister. Only one year younger than Iris, Daisy had the same mothering instinct, but with a much gentler touch. "What's her name?"

Jane shrugged her shoulders. She had really been counting on a boy. "I haven't thought of one yet, Sweetie."

Iris and Daisy exchanged looks. For each of their siblings, their parents had had names picked out from the moment of conception. How could this one be any different?

"Can I name her?" Rose asked.

Again, Jane shrugged her shoulders. All she really wanted to do was sleep. Tomorrow would be another busy day of managing her growing household. Iris and Daisy were mature enough to help, but they wouldn't be able to do it all while their father was at the market.

"Well, she won't be as pretty as the rest of us."

Iris glared at Rose in reproach, but her sister didn't take the hint.

"We could call her Pansy."

Jane shook her head. Even though her girls rarely interacted with the outside world, at one point they would. Pansy wasn't an option.

"How about Jasmine?" Daisy suggested. Again, Jane shook her head, already weary of the conversation. The girls didn't know what a television was, or about Disney movies, but Jane wasn't going to have her daughter named after one of the many princesses.

"We could name her Olive."

"Huh?" Iris and Daisy said in unison. "That's not a flower."

Rose pursed her lips and scowled. "Well, if she isn't pretty like a flower, maybe she shouldn't have a flower name."

"Look, Mama," Lily called from the door. Covered in mud from head to toe, she clutched a bouquet of mangled dandelions in her grubby little hand. "I brung tulips for baby."

Iris giggled and gingerly took the wilted flowers from her sister before she could stuff them in the baby's face.

"That's sweet, Lily." Carefully, she set them on the bedside table. "They are very... uh... pretty... Tulips."

Rose looked at the weeds in disgust, but knew better than to say anything in front of Iris. Lily had some strange ideas, even for a toddler. As she stared at the ragged posy, an idea started to form in her mind. "What about Tulip? We could call her Tulip."

At this point, Jane had started to drift off. The midwife placed the newborn in a bassinet beside the exhausted mother and nodded her agreement at the children. "I think your mother would like that very much. Now you children run outside and play. She needs to sleep."

Iris ushered her sisters out of the room. Lily went back to her mud pies, Rose picked up the reader she was working through, and Daisy started cleaning carrots and potatoes for their supper. For a fleeting moment, Iris wondered about the rest of the world, but the thoughts didn't last long. She had chores to do.

Chapter One

The email seemed innocent enough. The cry for help was obviously real. I could sense the emotion pouring from the sender, through her keyboard, across the intricate wires of the internet, and finally coming to rest in my laptop. The plea was heartfelt and urgent and I couldn't resist the little tug I felt at my heart. It wasn't like those other emails I had received, asking for pictures, professing true love, or insisting I'd won some lottery. Those ones were silly. Of course love transcends time, race, colour, and distance but even I won't be drawn in by false promises of love and affection. Besides, my sister Iris had warned me to be extra leery of internet scams, and I'm pretty sure that sending pictures to complete strangers was one of those dangers to be avoided.

This letter was different. The woman had lost her husband. Her son was in need of protection and her health was quickly deteriorating. She couldn't even trust her own family so she was offering a generous compensation plan for helping her in this dire predicament. Twenty-five percent of over five million dollars was nothing to scoff at, even if it did mean taking on the care of a child until he reached the age of majority.

The only personal information she was requesting was my full name, address, and telephone number, all things that could easily be found in a phonebook or through Canada 411. How she had managed to find my email address was a bit of a mystery, but with such easy access to the internet, it probably wasn't too difficult for someone who knew how. I'm glad she wrote to me and not someone who would take advantage of her unfortunate situation. Some people would simply delete the message— or worse. Others might take advantage of the money and leave her poor son to fend for himself, making them no better than this poor woman's seedy relatives.

I was a little concerned those relatives might find me, but I'm a Canadian citizen and protected by the government and banks here. If the money was transferred and her son came to live with me until appropriate arrangements could be made, I was certain things would eventually work themselves out. I read the email one more time to be sure she wasn't asking for personal banking information or credit card numbers. Each time I read this woman's message my eyes started to tear up and my heart fractured a tiny bit more. She seemed so desperate. Despite the poor grammar, strange word usage, distance, and obvious risk getting involved with an African state, I wanted to help.

Cautiously I responded to her email, choosing my words carefully:

Dear Mrs. Akiss,

I hope this letter finds you in good health and spirits. Upon receiving your heartfelt email, I decided I wanted to help you. You'll

Money, Masks & Madness

have to understand my nervousness in contacting you. Not everyone on the internet is honest, and so I will need proof of who you are, as well as the details regarding your family situation before we can proceed.

Sincerely,

Tulip Garden

I hesitated briefly before clicking the send button. If Iris found out I had responded, she would have something to say about it, but I knew in my heart I was doing the right thing. Since moving to the city, all I ever saw were people who are completely engrossed in their own lives. Selfish, materialistic, and so self-absorbed they are unable to see the pain and suffering of the world around them. I wasn't concerned about the money aspect of the message. Even though I'm not rich by anyone's standards, I always seem to manage with what I have. I was more worried about the state of her child and bringing him to a safe place to grow up.

When I first read the email, I looked up Cote d'Ivoire in West Africa to verify if this was a real plea for help. Indeed, the small country was in turmoil. If Mrs. Akiss couldn't care for her child because of her failing health, he needed to be removed from the country as soon as possible. I wasn't prepared to look after him, but I'm sure Youth Protection Services would be able to step in once he arrived. After all, they were established to protect children, weren't they?

I looked at the clock and realized I was going to be late for work if I didn't leave soon. After logging out of my email, I switched off my computer, slipped on my new two- inch wedge heels, grabbed my purse and keys, and headed out the door of my little apartment. Quietly, I pulled the stubborn door shut. My roommate Chaz was still sleeping and I didn't want to disturb him by slamming the door, although that would have been so much easier. Before locking up our apartment, I checked my oversized purse for the supply of fruit and snacks I kept handy to ensure I would have enough for the day ahead.

I lived a short walk from my work; on the way I passed by a few people who I knew were in need of support. Rather than dole out pennies, nickels, and dimes, I passed them a banana, apple, or granola bar. Depending on what was on the clearance rack, there was the possibility I could provide them with something more substantial, always keeping in mind they might not have the means to open a can or actually cook food.

"Good morning," I said to the liberally pierced teenage girl who sat with her back propped against a brick wall. Her hair was pulled back in greasy pigtails and she had her dog snuggled up on a blanket beside her. I handed her an apple and a biscuit for her dog. Noting he had water in the old margarine container, I didn't bother to fill it from my water bottle.

She nodded, accepted the treats, and I moved on, my heart feeling a bit lighter knowing I could offer something, regardless of how small it was, to ease the burdens of her day. For every homeless, down-on-his-luck person I ran into, I offered up fruit, cereal bars, and biscuits for their dogs. Each one thanked me in his own way, accustomed to seeing me on my way to work. I didn't judge them. How could I? Not knowing where they had come from or how they had arrived.

Money, Masks & Madness

I opened the door to The Macabre Mercantile to find my boss, Alistair, in fine form this morning. He was ranting at his sculptors, correcting the make-up artists, and generally throwing a temper tantrum better suited to a two year old.

"You're late," he snarled at me, his British accent making the words sound clipped and harsh.

I shrugged out of my loose-fitting sweater, hung it with my purse on a hook, and turned to smile at him. Working with Alistair had proven to be quite a challenge, but I was starting to see through his surly attitude to the creative perfectionist inside. I wasn't late. I knew for a fact he set his watch eight minutes fast; he was paranoid about missing a deadline when it came down to the last few minutes. The clock on the wall read eight o'clock on the dot.

"Missing your coffee?" I asked as I made my way over to the "coffee station".

Alistair had a serious addiction, which he pretty much forced on all his employees. He loved coffee, the stronger the better. Depending on his mood, he might ask for a dark roast or something a bit milder. Regardless, he drank about ten cups of various flavours, strengths and blends, throughout the day. He was particular about how each should look and taste. If I didn't get it right, it was dumped and recreated. The complexity of his machine could rival any major specialty coffee shop. I guess having worked at the local Starbucks made me an easy fit for this job. In fact, to be honest, it was probably my only qualification in getting it.

"Come on, Petal, I haven't got all day." Alistair's accent was a bit annoying at the best of times, but his impatience made it so much worse—that and the fact that he couldn't seem to bring himself to call me by name. I don't know if it was because he couldn't be bothered to remember it or if he was making fun of my given name. It wasn't like I chose it.

Determined to get it right on the first attempt, I made adjustments to the machine, measured out the coffee and flipped the switch. As the shiny contraption chugged, and burbled, releasing a belch of steam with a gurgling moan, I sighed in relief. At least I wouldn't have to try that part again. Even the milk froth decided to cooperate this time. Carefully, I scooped it over the steamy coffee and managed to manipulate the froth to form a little swirl. Success!

"Happy?" I asked. I swear the man looked at me disdainfully, but accepted the mug anyway. As he turned away, I resisted the urge to stick my tongue out at him. I needed this job, at least until something better came along.

Realizing he was marching away without me, I quickly followed, cursing my choice of footwear. My older sister, Rose, insisted I needed to join the grown-up world and wear heels, but my job required me to be on my feet all day. Being a personal assistant to one of the top latex mask and make-up men in the horror business was rather demanding.

"No, no, no." I arrived in time to hear Alistair's voice echoing through the latex room. "He's supposed to be scary, evil, the stuff of nightmares. This thing looks like something a kid would snuggle with at night."

"But, sir, the client wants—"

"Do it again."

Money, Masks & Madness

Paige looked down at the grotesque zombie head in front of her, made a snarl with her fuchsia painted lips, and flipped her purple tipped hair over her shoulder, all the while glaring at her employer. Alistair didn't pay attention. Instead, he marched towards the next workstation, with me following close behind. Her work was scary, but if I were honest about it, I had seen her do better.

"I hire imbeciles," Alistair muttered as he surveyed the mask in front of him. Derek was studying his work and frowning. He told me yesterday he thought it was shaping into one of his better pieces. "Blossom here could probably create something more imaginative than this."

I narrowed my eyes, pretty certain that was an insult.

I looked at Derek's creation and suppressed a shudder. It might not be the most imaginative creature Alistair had ever seen, but with its popping eyes, drooping mouth, and hacked-off nose, it wasn't something I would like to come across in my travels. Even though I saw these things every day, I wasn't immune to their gruesome countenance. In fact, they confirmed how twisted and sick the human mind really is.

"Blast it, where is that girl now?" Alistair had obviously moved on while I was busy scrutinizing Derek's work. Without hesitation I lurched forward, bumping into the heavily tattooed Dieter at the next work station, causing him to scramble to catch a multitude of paints before they landed on the floor. Luckily, they were all closed tight.

"Sorry," I muttered, handing him back a paint tube that had landed at my feet.

"Buttercup, let's go. I need a pencil."

I ducked under Dieter's arm, not a difficult feat, since he stood well over six feet tall, and caught up with my boss. I handed him the desired pencil and had a pad of paper at hand, just in case.

"I'm not sure why I keep you around."

I wasn't sure why he kept me around either, but chose to believe his question was rhetorical. The employment agency generally sent me to walk dogs, clean houses and pour coffee. This was my first experience as a personal assistant.

Alistair Green is demanding and rather… well… it's probably best if you meet him for yourself," Grace, my caseworker, tried to explain. "He's had a hard time keeping staff, but he's in a crunch and pretty much willing to take anyone."

I wasn't sure I liked the sound of that last part, but decided I would try the position anyway. I needed the work. My rent was due, Kraft Dinner only has so much nutritional value, and my sisters were constantly chastising me about my inability to keep a job for more than a month.

With a grimace, I brought my thoughts back to the present. Alistair was impatient with my tendency to drift off into the world of my imagination. If I let myself, I would be indulging in a rewritten script of how my placement interview went: one where I had a backbone and didn't allow caseworkers who didn't know a thing about me to make derogatory comments they didn't think I would understand.

"You keep me around for my good looks," I quipped and immediately regretted it.

Alistair frowned at me, handed over his coffee mug, and took the pencil. He leaned forward and made a few quick strokes on the drafting table.

"It needs to look more like this." He studied his own work and nodded with approval. "What do you think, Sunshine?"

It took me a moment to realize he was asking my opinion. I gave myself a mental shake and rested my eyes on the gruesome display before me. Shuddering in distaste, I searched for the right words. "It's… uh… well…"

"Perfect!" Alistair handed the pencil back and retrieved his coffee. An amused smile flickered across his handsome features as he sauntered towards his next victim.

For the past two weeks we had followed the same routine. Alistair would demand some fancy coffee; I would brew first one cup, which was usually unacceptable, followed by a second, which, if I were lucky, would be "good enough". Following that we would make our rounds, like doctors in a hospital, except these patients were far from being saved. The more gruesome and horrendous the masks, the more he liked them. Alistair always complimented those I hated most and criticized the ones I could actually bear to look at. In general, the place looked like some kind of weird and twisted burial ground for monsters. One of the artists told me this wasn't always the case, but I had my doubts on the matter.

"Chop, chop, people, we have a deadline to meet."

Did he really just say that? I shook my head in wonder, thinking that was something people would say in the movies, not real life. Of course, this was about as close to movie making as I would ever get, since they were creating bits and pieces for the upcoming zombie apocalypse movie, "Dread the Dead".

Paige had already started to dismantle her creation. She peeled the "skin" from the ceramic bust, tossed it in the corner with the rest of the cast-offs, and set to work recreating the image Alistair had sketched weeks ago. Although I tried to ignore her, I could see her glaring at me as I passed by. Perhaps if I had grimaced in distaste, she might have been making minor adjustments instead of recreating the mask altogether. Considering the creature in question only had a passing role, I couldn't believe how much detail Alistair required.

"Come, Buttercup, I have a list for you."

I sighed, knowing precisely what would be on that list. I would be spending my afternoon running around the streets of Montreal, picking up his dry cleaning, St Viateur's bagels, and quite possibly, venturing into Chinatown for some obscure ingredient he had to have.

Chapter Two

"Why do you do this to yourself?" Rose asked, as she ordered her deli sandwich. Since I moved out of our apartment a year ago, we tried to get together at least once a week. I would tell her my woes and she would criticize my fashion sense, choice of job, and living arrangements.

I ignored her and ordered my meal. I never could get used to the selection of processed foods available on every corner. Instead of a rubbery meat sandwich, I chose a salad which contained more iceberg lettuce than actual vegetables.

"No dressing, please. And a slice of goat's cheese."

"Seriously, you deserve better than this. You're smart enough to do anything you want." Rose picked up her tray and continued chastising me on her way to our table. "I mean, look at Iris. She put herself through university, became a teacher, and is now happily married. Don't you want that for yourself?"

"Iris is seven years older than me. I'm not even close to wanting to be married. Besides, you're not doing your dream job either."

"You would have to point that out," Rose grumbled. "I'm working my way towards it—there's a difference. Journalism is tricky. It's about who you know and being in the right place at the right time. At least I have a goal in sight."

I picked through the wilted lettuce; my salad looked sad and limp even though I had watched it being made fresh in front of me. "The only one of us even close to being perfectly happy is Lily. She loves her little hobby farm. I'm glad she moved to the country, even though I miss her."

"Well, I'm glad we joined civilization. Can you imagine all that we would be missing if we were still living in that buggy old cabin? I find it so hard to believe people actually pay to live like that. Mind you, it's only for a week or two at time, and they probably have satellite television, so it's not really the same at all, is it?"

I smiled wryly. Our childhood home had hardly been old or buggy. My memories were sketchy, but held a picture of quaint rustic beauty, not the grim and desolate picture Rose would paint. "I guess not."

Rose studied me intently, momentarily silent, making me wonder what she was thinking. I'm not overly talkative to begin with, but today I was feeling a bit sullen. Perhaps it was the disturbing email I had received this morning. I couldn't get that poor woman's plight out of my head.

"What's up with you, cranky pants?"

"I'm all right. Maybe all the monsters are getting to me. It's a creepy kind of place to work." I couldn't tell Rose what was really bothering me, she would run off and tell Iris and Daisy. I would never hear the end of it.

"You have to admit you have an exciting job though. Not everyone can say they've worked so closely with Alistair Green. It's too bad you're nothing but a gopher. Even answering the phones would be a step up."

Money, Masks & Madness

"True."

I contemplated the withered grape tomato I had just eaten. It was flavourless, probably because it had been sitting in the refrigerator for so long. I guess it was time to visit Lily. Even though her organic veggies wouldn't keep for long, they were the most flavourful treats, much better than anything you could find in the city.

"And, he's not bad to look at, either."

I pushed my plate away, unable to finish the unappetizing meal. Alistair was mildly attractive, but I wasn't about to admit that to Rose.

"You're not serious? He's... so... so... British-looking. All pale skin, big ears, and wide eyes." This, of course was a lie. Alistair is an attractive man but I couldn't think of my employer like that.

"You could do worse." Rose took a bite of her sandwich and chewed thoughtfully. "At the very least, you should consider it."

In my head, I took my pathetic salad and dumped it over my sister's head. In reality, I flung a solitary piece of lettuce in Rose's direction, being careful to miss her.

"If you think he's such a good catch, you go after him. I'll even introduce you. Then you can spend your days making coffee, fetching corpse heads, and searching for the best ingredients to make rotten flesh."

"Oh no, he pays people for that."

"Funny."

"I am."

I laughed. As annoying as Rose could be, she had a pretty decent sense of humour. "I need to get back. He likes me to be there for his rounds. I guess I'm some sort of fright-o-metre. The more I find something repulsive, the more he likes it."

"You really need a new job."

"Yup, I do. But until I find something better, I guess I'll stick this one out. I feel kind of bad for him. The employment agency said he has a hard time keeping staff."

Rose stared at me for a moment. I could see her mind clicking away, trying to decide whether or not she should say what she was thinking. It didn't take her long to open her mouth—she wasn't one for keeping her thoughts to herself. "He has a hard time because he's looking for a wife, not an assistant."

"You're crazy. That doesn't even make any sense." I tried to ignore the niggling feeling that she might be right. I needed this job, not just so I could pay my bills, but because I had difficulty committing to any one thing. I was using this position to prove to myself I could stay focused and build a career.

"Think about it. You make coffee, pick up his dry cleaning, keep his office tidy, sort out his crap… you're more like a wife than a secretary."

"I'm a Personal Assistant—I get paid to do personal stuff for him."

Rose arched one perfectly sculpted eyebrow. "Like a wife."

I shook my head. There was no point in arguing. Once Rose had an idea in her head, it was nearly impossible to shake it free.

The afternoon rounds with Alistair proved to be uneventful until he was interrupted midway through his inspection of the latest masks.

Money, Masks & Madness

"This place is disgusting. How do you sleep at night? How do any of you sleep at night?" The booming voice, twin in accent to Alistair's, could only belong to one person. According to Paige, Adam Green was a younger, better-looking, more vibrant version of his older brother. Known for being a bit of a playboy, he was also involved in the movie industry, but his goal was to play the leading man, not the decomposing dead guy.

The transformation in the studio was incredible. It was like there had been an invasion; except this time of the living sort, as opposed to the undead or living dead or whatever the coolest catch-phrase was for zombies. Seeing this much life in the studio even made Paige pause to take note. She was one of the more focused sculptors on staff which would account for her unique and realistic pieces. I was certain it was because she had an unusual affinity for the dead. Her specialty was vampires, but she could pull off a pretty good zombie in a pinch.

I tried to get a look at the owner of the disembodied voice, but there were too many living heads in the way. Paige gave me a little nudge when Alistair started moving—my cue to follow the man, lest he take his temper out on his creative staff and not his assistant. From the look on her face, it was obvious Paige wasn't in the mood to recreate another of his monsters with such a tight deadline looming.

Following him like the lost puppy I was, I watched as Alistair slapped his brother on the back and waited for the younger man to turn around. Briefly, I wondered if Adam would have the same overbearing, insensitive manner his older brother did. When he did turn, I caught my breath in surprise. Where Alistair's face was all sharp angles,

Adam's was rough-hewn edges—the kind you expect to see on a ruggedly attractive movie star. Alistair's hair was auburn, limp, and straight; Adam's was dark, thick, and curly. Dark eyes, dark hair and tanned skin. He wasn't at all what I had been expecting, even though I had been forewarned by Paige.

"You could put on some music, liven things up a bit in here. It's deathly silent." Adam chuckled at his own joke, but Alistair just stared at him, his face expressionless.

"We like it like this. The silence is soothing and helps my artists focus on their inner demons so they can create unique sculptures. This movie is going to get me an award for best costume design. I know it. I can taste it."

"I'm afraid what you're tasting is latex pâté, my friend." Again, Adam laughed at his joke, ignoring the quiet of everyone else in the workspace. No one dared joke about this project. It meant too much to Alistair and everyone else on his team.

"Can I get you a coffee, Mr. Green?" I asked in an attempt to break the silence. Stepping out from behind my boss, I looked directly up into Adam's brown eyes. My knees gave a little quiver and my mouth went unexpectedly dry. Paige was right: Adam Green was delicious to look at.

He smiled down at me and shook his head. "Well, would you look at that? A wood sprite. Who'd a thunk it?"

Alistair took a step forward, his body language indicating he was unhappy with his brother's choice of words. "She's *my employee* and you'll do well to stay away from her."

"She's a fine looking ginger-cat and I'm pretty sure she's fair game."

"She's a child."

Money, Masks & Madness

As much as I thought I should appreciate this suddenly protective side of Alistair, once again, I felt like I was being insulted. I had left my childhood behind, long ago, on a country road. The last thing I needed from anyone was protection.

"I'm neither a child nor a cat." I stepped between the two men, gauging their level of hostility. Both of them looked ready to explode and I was quite certain I actually had nothing to do with it despite being the topic of their argument. "How do you take your coffee, Mr. Green?"

Adam looked at me for a long moment. I'm sure he was measuring my spirit and strength with that one glance. "I don't drink coffee."

"Figures," I muttered quietly as I turned away. I could have sworn I saw a glimmer of a smile on Alistair's face.

Wanting nothing more than to escape the two of them, I made a dash for the door, tripping over wayward body parts in my haste. They could continue their argument without an audience; I had work to do.

Jennifer Bogart

Chapter Three

I stared up at the sky through the living room window of my apartment, trying to figure out how I had managed to get where I was. Life had started out simple enough. Just me and my family, living a modest country life and not demanding anything in return. After fifteen years of living in what Rose calls "civilization", I still feel I don't quite fit in. People know things I don't. They refer to television shows, music, and movie clips in every day conversation, making me feel uneducated and somehow lacking when I have no frame of reference for what they are talking about. Even though our mother had moved us into suburbia, she had continued to shelter us from outside sources for as long as possible. We had never owned a television or a computer.

I try to keep up. I try to look as though I know what they are talking about. The interesting things I have to draw from are classic books my mother had used as homeschooling tools. I could almost recite "A Tale of Two Cities", most of Mark Twain's work, and the poetry of Wordsworth and Poe. Perhaps I was drawn to work with Alistair because of his connection to all things modern. Granted, he made me feel a bit like "Alice in Wonderland"—never really knowing what's right or wrong. Eat this. Drink that. And don't pay any attention to the cat.

Aren't zombies the next big thing? Everyone was talking about them and the upcoming zombie apocalypse. Sure, it was probably all in fun, and no one really believed it would happen. But what if a small part of them did? It sure would explain a few interesting things I had seen since moving to the city.

I shifted my weight on the couch, trying to find a comfortable spot between the thin cushions and jutting springs without losing sight of the night sky. Granted, all I could see were smoggy clouds, city lights, and the occasional airplane. It might be the same sky that had sheltered me my entire life, but here in the city, it didn't feel the same. Something was missing, and I'm sure it was hidden out there, beyond the stars so cleverly camouflaged by the illuminated city.

The lock to my apartment clicked, followed by the doorknob jiggling as my roommate, Chaz, leaned heavily on it to push it open. We lived in one of those historically protected buildings in desperate need of updating. With the heat and humidity of summer, the old wooden door had swelled to the point of barely fitting in its frame. The landlord had promised to fix the offensive object, but hadn't gotten around to it. I was fairly certain I could do it myself, but the idea horrified Chaz. He didn't feel comfortable doing any sort of repairs in a building he didn't own. Not that he would ever be able to own one with his current salary.

Chaz was a wanna-be model, slash actor, slash fashion designer. Sweet and sensitive, he was more in touch with his feminine side than I have ever been. Quirky as he was, he's probably the best friend I have ever had.

Money, Masks & Madness

I thought about the day I met him, purely by accident. Daisy was working nights at the Montreal Children's Hospital and I was meeting her for breakfast after her shift. Because she was tired, we decided to meet at a café in the plaza across the street from the hospital. Unfortunately, it was a busy place, with nowhere to sit. In an attempt to be nice, I had already ordered her coffee and favourite pastry, but was left standing in the middle of the café, holding the full tray, desperately searching for a place to sit.

"Here, you can sit with me."

I looked over to see a young man smiling in my direction. Plaid trousers matched with a sparkly shirt had me questioning his sanity.

"I'm almost finished and that tray looks like it's getting heavy."

I looked down at the food I was carrying. It didn't weigh much, but the awkwardness of standing in the middle of a crowded room was starting to get to me. Without much thought, I set down the tray and took the seat across from him.

"Thank you." Fairly new to the city, I wasn't used to the friendly camaraderie of strangers.

"I'm Chaz Selinzky." He reached his hand across the table and took mine in a firm handshake.

"Tulip Garden," I responded quietly. Usually when I told people my name, they did one of three things. They commented on how pretty it was, how unusual it was, or they questioned it. I braced myself for what I knew was coming.

"Nice to meet you, Tulip. Are you from Montreal?" He leaned back in his chair, looking relaxed, and I couldn't help but notice his bright blue eyes sparkling with genuine curiosity.

"Not really. My sister and I moved in a few weeks ago. She's a journalist. Well, sort of a journalist. It will take time, but she'll get there." I knew I was babbling, but I couldn't help myself. He sat there, looking interested in every word I uttered. All my life I had lived in the shadow of my more dynamic sisters. Sitting here with this stranger, I felt for a moment that I was the only person who mattered in his world.

He nodded and took a sip of his coffee. "Have you managed to find work yet?"

I shook my head. I had an appointment with an employment agency later that day. Iris had insisted I start there, given my limited education. Daisy and I were meeting to go over possible interview questions so I could make a good first impression.

Chaz reached across the table and handed me a business card. "If you need any help, try these guys. They're good."

I took the card from him and noted the name of the agency. It was for models and actors. "Uh... I don't... this isn't . . ."

"Not what you're looking for?" He shook his head while offering a rueful smile. "You should be. You're gorgeous with all that ginger hair and your slim build. A little on the short side, but I think that can be worked around."

"I'm full of freckles." I blurted out the first thing that came to mind. I didn't know this guy, and here he was telling me how beautiful I was. If Rose were sitting here, she'd think she'd been transported to a heavenly dimension.

"Listen, Buttercup, I'm a model and I've worked with hundreds of beautiful women. The moment I laid eyes on you I could see your appeal. Your soul shines through with every breath you take and every word you utter. Modeling and acting are about more than looking good, they're also about looking right. I've never met anyone more right."

I should have been flattered, instead I felt unbelievably awkward.

"Uh… thank you."

He smiled the kind of smile that reaches past the lips, glitters in the eyes and becomes part of your heart. "You're welcome."

I may have blushed, but I know I returned his smile, taking in his bleached blond hair, pretty blue eyes, and interesting fashion choices. The guy was self-confident and sure of himself. I wanted to be like him when I grew up.

"This heat is killing me," Chaz announced dramatically, drawing me out of my reverie. He set a couple of grease-soaked bags, that looked like they came from the local Chinese takeout place, on our 1970's era Formica table, and tossed his keys into a bowl on the counter. The man might be complaining about the heat, but his satiny yellow muscle shirt looked cool and dry.

"It's not so bad."

I got up from the couch and came over to inspect the bags. Yup—Chinese takeout and not the good stuff either. I shook my head, but didn't say anything. At least I wouldn't have to cook tonight. What I couldn't understand was why anyone would purchase "fake" Chinese food when a plethora of the real thing was available up the street. It wasn't any more expensive, but you had to be willing to walk a few extra blocks.

"How was your day?" I asked as I started to remove the soggy boxes from the bags.

Chaz washed his hands in the kitchen sink, dried them, and pulled out two plates from the drying rack. "Oh, you know, the usual. It's hard working with people who don't or can't appreciate your art."

I tried not to giggle. "What art? I thought you were working at the dépanneur to help Roger out."

"I was."

"So what "art" are you talking about? Your creative pitch for beer? The artful display of chocolate bars you created?" I fanned my hands in front of me, adding flair to my words.

"Tsk. You wouldn't understand."

Knowing I wouldn't, I let the subject drop.

"How was your day at the monster factory?"

"Oh, you know, the usual. Body parts littered everywhere. A little blood, a little gore. Nothing out of the ordinary." I grimaced at the deep fried chicken balls slathered in red sauce. They didn't look at all appetizing. Gingerly, I pushed the box aside and selected another. This one was a vegetable dish, a little slimy, but it would have to do.

"I heard Adam Green is in town. Did he stop in to see his creepy brother?" Chaz was carefully picking his way through his meal, using chopsticks even though he was clearly struggling with them. I couldn't understand how he ate so much and never gained any weight. Tall, lean, and model good-looking, he ate what he wanted when he wanted, and never had an extra ounce on him to show for it. Not that I had to worry about it either, but I didn't eat half of what he did.

I pushed my plate away, disgusted for the second time that day by the food choices offered in the city. We have access to the most delicious things imaginable, so I couldn't figure out why Chaz chose such horrible, almost synthetic things to eat.

"He came in for a few minutes."

Chaz put his chopsticks down on his plate and nearly jumped out of his chair. "I don't believe this! If I hadn't asked, you wouldn't have told me!" He started pacing around the little apartment, moving from kitchen to living room and back again in ten easy strides. "You're something else, I tell you!"

"It's not a big deal, you know. My sisters come around here all the time and you never get that excited."

"Your sisters haven't been on the covers of magazines and in movies. They aren't up and coming in the industry."

I shrugged my shoulders. "Well, the way I see it, people are people. Famous, infamous, nobodies—we're all the same on the inside."

"Right," Chaz picked up his dishes and carried them to the sink. "But on the outside we're nothing alike. That's where the Adam Greens and Bethany Campbells of the world come in. If we were all the same, life would be boring."

"I didn't mean we're all carbon copies of each other. I simply meant that deep down inside, we all come from the same place. A place that needs to be nurtured, loved, and encouraged. A place that needs other people, whether we like it or not. Of course we're not all exactly the same, that would be awful."

"You know, Tulip. Sometimes I don't understand a word you're trying to say. It's like you're talking all gobbledygook when what you're really trying to express is something deep and philosophical. I'm too shallow to follow your deep sense of self."

I grabbed my own plate and tossed the remainder of my supper in the garbage before dropping it into the sink for washing. Of course he'd pull the "I don't get what you're trying to say" avoidance tactic. Chaz's life revolved around his next big break, handsome boys, pretty girls, and exotic places.

"You know, Chaz," I mimicked his tone. "Sometimes you're such an ass I can hardly stand to be in the same room with you."

"I'm teasing you, Buttercup. You should know me better than that by now."

He studied me carefully from his position across the room, and even though I turned my face away, I knew it was too late. We'd been friends for too long for him not to see when I was feeling out of sorts.

"What's wrong? This isn't like you."

I didn't want to talk about my day, my feelings of inferiority, or the disturbing email I had received this morning. At least, I didn't want to talk about it with people whose lives were on the fast train to fame and success. For the briefest moment, I thought Rose and Chaz would work well together. They had the same quest for all things beautiful in common.

"Just a long day," I said quietly. "I'm going to take a relaxing bath, snuggle up with a good book, and go to bed early so I can start fresh tomorrow."

Chapter Four

When I was a child, we had an old claw-foot, porcelain bathtub. You could fill it deep, sink into the luxuriating warmth, and let your worries drift away in a froth of scented bubbles. My apartment has a dinky little tub, scarred with rust stains, and surrounded by chipped tiles. I might not have been able to do much about the physicality of the situation, but a few candles, some vanilla bubble bath, and soft music easily changed the ambiance in the room. With closed eyes, I sank into the comforting warmth, enjoying the contrast of the heated water and the cool bubbles as they popped in a fizzing sensation on my skin. Beside me, on the closed toilet seat, was a glass of wine and the book I was currently reading. This was my little slice of Utopia.

A sharp rap at the door, followed by a click, and the squeak of hinges had me sinking lower into the cover of bubbles. Chaz poked first his head in the door, followed quickly by the rest of his lean body. Briefly, I considered chastising him, but I knew there wasn't any point. We had had the privacy conversation countless times before. The fact that he considered me to be no different than any of his model friends hadn't helped my ego any, even if it was meant to put me at ease. We had been sharing an apartment for a year now, which in his mind meant there was no need for privacy. I'd seen the kind of women he was attracted to and I definitely didn't fit into the category.

"What?" I asked. The sooner he got what he needed, the sooner I could get back to relaxing.

He looked at me steadily with those piercing blue eyes. If I didn't know better, I'd think he wore contact lenses to intensify their colour.

"I was just thinking."

Chaz "just thinking" inevitably leads to trouble. His ideas are as flamboyant as his clothing. Whenever they include me, I usually regret getting involved, but by that time it's too late. Once he convinced me to model for one of his painter friends. As instructed, I wore jeans and a plain white t-shirt. The final product didn't resemble me at all. The woman in the painting had huge breasts, wide hips, and a come-hither smile. In comparison, I am scrawny and completely lacking in feminine curves. I've seen skinny men with bigger breasts than I have.

"Hmmm . . ." I didn't want to know what scheme he was devising in that head of his. I wanted to relax in my bath with my wine and book. I didn't think that was too much to ask for.

"I'm in a fashion show in a couple of weeks and they are short one female model."

"No."

"C'mon, Tulip. You'd be perfect for it."

I sank deeper into the water, making sure the bubbles covered all my relevant parts. "I'm flattered, but no. I'm too short and flat as a board. Probably not at all what they're looking for."

"You're exactly what they're looking for. A bit too skinny for my tastes, but I think you'd do in a pinch."

Money, Masks & Madness

How had we gone from me being a "perfect for it" to "you'd do in a pinch"?

"No. I'm busy."

"You don't even know when it is."

I smiled at that. "I'm too busy with my job. It's exhausting."

"Which is precisely why you should consider this gig. Think about it—a change of pace, new faces, and best of all, a bit of extra money for your effort." He ventured further into the bathroom and sat on the toilet seat, holding my wine in one hand and the book in the other.

I reached for my glass, being careful to keep the bubbles strategically placed, not the easiest feat, given the shallowness of the tub. It might have been my imagination, but I could have sworn Chaz turned away just enough to keep the glass out of my grasp.

"Give me my wine."

"Say you'll do it." He chuckled, his eyes crinkled, and the shadow of a dimple appeared in his left cheek.

I settled back into the tub with much sloshing of water, unfortunately displacing the cover of white foam. "I can do without the wine," I lied.

He turned back, handed me the glass, and continued to stare at me. I glanced down to ensure my pseudo covering was still in place, and back up to see him trying to smother a grin. He couldn't maintain a straight face for long.

"C'mon, Tulip. It'll be fun. Just a quick jaunt down a runway—even then it's more of an aisle—and you're finished. The girl you'll be replacing is about your size."

"Why can't she do it?" Maybe she was sick or had a family emergency. If either were the case, I would hate to see the show be a failure because one person couldn't be there. The longer he stared at me, the more I felt myself leaning towards an unfortunate "yes".

"Well... uh . . ."

His hesitation spoke volumes to me. Perhaps she had backed out because it wasn't the kind of show she wanted to be in. I knew Chaz took some pretty big risks, but he's young and single, and doesn't much care about his reputation provided each gig gets him one step closer to his final goal.

I took a sip of the cool wine and waited for his reply.

To my surprise, he blushed slightly. "Her... uh... she was too... big for the outfit."

"I don't get it."

He shifted, looked at me steadily, turned away and returned to let his gaze travel the length of my body which was now partially revealed. Cheap bubble bath doesn't have staying power. It was my turn to blush, and I'm sure my cheeks were brighter than my carroty hair.

"Her boobs were too big," he blurted out as he stood and backed away from the tub. The book landed on the floor with a loud clatter, making me jump and causing the water to slosh over the sides and onto the floor. I looked in dismay as the pages began to soak up the wet.

"Her—? Oh, never mind." Now that I had my glass of wine, the best I could do was cross my arms over my own breasts. "If I tell you I'll think about it, will you leave me in peace?"

Chaz nodded, grinning wickedly. "That's all I needed to hear. I'll call Mia and let her know."

Before I could contradict him, he ducked out of the room and quietly closed the door behind him. I sat up in the tub and reached over the side, knowing it was too late to rescue the book, but not willing to let it sit in the puddle any longer. No sooner did I have the book in my hand then Chaz swung open the door.

"One more thing," he said as I clung precariously to the side of the tub, "your co-worker Paige will also be there. I thought I should let you know."

What did I care if Paige was there? As quickly as he entered the room, he left again. Leaving me with a soggy book, a lukewarm bath and not enough wine in the world to get me through what I had been coerced into doing.

I woke slowly, listening for birds and other sounds of nature, while knowing the likelihood was slim to none. Even though it was summer in the city, and I was lucky enough to live in a walk-up with windows that actually opened, the wildlife sounds tended to be muffled by the traffic. The rumble of an airplane flying low overhead forced me from my reverie. Glancing at the clock, I realized it was barely six in the morning. I had plenty of time to get ready for work and even check my email. I was wondering if Mrs. Akiss had received my message.

After steeping some organic peach and ginger tea (compliments of Lily's hobby farm), I took my mug and headed for my laptop. My sisters had pooled their money together for my last birthday to give it to me as a gift. At first I thought they were crazy. I didn't even own a television, what would I want with a computer? Rose had set me up with internet access, which in my mind was one more bill to pay. Iris had shown me how to access email (probably so she would have yet another way of keeping tabs on me), and Daisy tried to get me hooked on Facebook. The Facebook thing didn't really work for me though. I need to be face to face with people. I need to listen to the tones of their voices and see the subtle nuances in their expressions. Typewritten letters on the page leave so many open interpretations. I have a hard enough time reading people when they're in front of me: on Facebook, it's practically impossible.

As the machine took a few minutes to run through the usual start up motions, I sat quietly and gazed out the window, watching nothing in particular. From our living room, I could clearly see the street below me, where a few early risers were jogging past, pushing strollers, or balancing brief cases. It was a fairly quiet street for Montreal, with little vehicular traffic. The bus stop was at the end of the street and few cars passed through the narrow lane. Those that did were usually residents in search of a coveted parking spot.

A flicker on the screen drew my attention and I realized the laptop was ready to go. With a click of the mouse, I pulled up my email, entered the password, and watched as the messages loaded. Three messages were unusual for me. Most days, when I bothered to check, I was lucky if there was one waiting from Iris. Usually, it would be to chastise me about not returning a phone call, or checking in with her. She's a regular mother-hen and I love her dearly, but she seems to forget that one of the reasons I didn't move in with her was so that I could have a bit of breathing room.

The email entitled "Dear Friend" caught my attention first. I clicked on it and skimmed through the message.

Money, Masks & Madness

Mrs. Akiss understood my need for more information and went into a detailed report of how her late husband had practically been murdered during the 2010-2011 Civil War. Although he had invested well, and theirs was a wealthy family, they started to slip into ruin as his family attempted to steal her son's inheritance. With her failing health, she was afraid for the safety and welfare of her child. Currently, the money her husband left her was tied up in trust for their son, to safeguard it from his relatives. She needed help to release those funds so she could send her child to a place of safety as she lay dying in her hospital bed.

My heart was breaking for her. How terrible for her and her young son to live in constant fear after the death of her husband. Quickly, I wrote back, hoping she would understand I wasn't after her money, and that my primary concern was for the care and well-being of herself and her child. Perhaps if she came to Canada, she could get the medical treatment she needed to see her child grow into adulthood. All she had to do was send me a few more details regarding her health issues and I might be able to find a doctor willing to take on her case. I did live in a city that housed some of the finest medical research facilities. With UQAM and McGill University right around the corner, surely someone would understand this poor woman's plight, take pity on her, and offer up their medical expertise.

Dear Mrs. Akiss,

I am devastated to hear of your dire predicament and wish to help both you and your son. Would it be possible for you to send me a detailed medical report? I have access to wonderful doctors who might be able to give you the necessary medical treatment so you can care for your child yourself. After all, a child needs his mother more than he needs millions of dollars.

Sincerely,

Tulip Garden

I checked through the message for typos and spelling mistakes and sent it off through the mysterious wires of the internet. Hopefully, it wasn't too late for Mrs. Akiss to seek medical help for her various ailments.

I was so engrossed in my musings, I barely noticed when Chaz wandered out of his bedroom wearing nothing but a pair of loose-fitting boxers with pink poodles splattered all over them. He smiled sleepily and headed straight to the fridge.

"Why are you up so early?"

"Audition this morning. Have to go to the gym first so my muscles are good and defined."

"Right." I shook my head. If it wasn't his muscles, it was his hair, or his skin, or his teeth needing whitening. He was a high maintenance kind of guy.

"Love letters?" he asked, nodding his head towards the computer.

"Of course." I wasn't about to share the details of my correspondence with Mrs. Akiss quite yet. Chaz was sweet, but he wasn't exactly the "giving kind". No doubt he would make a comment about how far away she was and that I wouldn't really be able to help her, so why bother trying.

He raised an eyebrow at my response and turned his attention back to the contents in the fridge. "Want an omelet?"

"Sure, sounds good."

"Wanna make it? I always burn them."

Right. I logged out of my email, turned off the computer, and stood to stretch. Of course I would make the omelets. I didn't think Chaz even knew how to turn on the oven. All the while I was cooking, I was waiting for him to bring up that fashion show, but he didn't. I'm not sure if I was grateful or not, but I was definitely curious.

Jennifer Bogart

Chapter Five

"Did you see that?"

"She's such a flake."

"Oh. My. God. I would be totally embarrassed."

I glanced over at the women in the coffee shop, knowing they were talking about me. They didn't even have the decency to lower their voices.

"Ignore them, Tulip, they aren't worth it." I could see Daisy was upset as she attempted to dry my white blouse with her napkin. I swatted her hands away. I could take care of myself. Her words were probably said as much for her as they were for me.

"I know." Dabbing at my coffee stained, semi-transparent shirt, I tried to take my sister's advice.

"I can't believe she's still sitting there, like nothing happened." The brunette took a sip of her coffee and continued to stare rudely.

Her partner shook her head in disdain. "I would be so out of here. It's like she's from the backwoods of nowhere."

Daisy's eyes grew wide and then narrowed surreptitiously. I knew that look and was tempted to duck under the polished wood table. Sweet as she was, no one messed with Daisy's little sisters.

"Let it go," I pleaded. "They don't know what they're talking about. Besides, it's true. I should be embarrassed. I'm so clumsy. I think it's these stupid shoes."

I stuck out my foot, nearly tripping a man who walked by carrying a tray laden with drinks for his family. Luckily, he managed to step out of the way. The only thing preventing any spillage was the plastic lids on the take-out cups. The women beside us didn't bother to hide their snickers.

"Rose insisted I needed proper shoes, so she bought me these things. After nearly a week, they're still too hard to walk in."

Daisy and I studied the shoes. They were simple. Brown, with a two inch wedge heel, they looked comfortable and stylish with my snug-fitting jeans and short-sleeved blouse. Only, if I had a choice, I would be barefoot. Unfortunately, that wasn't an option in the city.

"You're being silly, Tulip. You'll get the hang of them."

I surveyed the coffee shop, wondering why Iris had insisted everyone meet her here. Unlike her usual self, she was late by about ten minutes. Both Lily and Rose had yet to make an appearance and I doubted our mother had even been invited. If so, we would be gathered in her little house, right outside of the city. Having such a formal family gathering was unusual and I was feeling particularly on edge.

"Oh, there's Rose," I muttered.

I dropped my head forward, letting my red hair cascade around my face. Of all my sisters, I had the most difficulty with Rose. It was almost as though, in her perfection, Rose couldn't tolerate the existence of my imperfections. My four older sisters were blessed with our mother's classic good looks. Blond hair, ranging from pin straight (Rose) to curly (Lily), they were of average height, slim but curvy, and graceful in their movements. They all shared varying hues of blue eyes: all slightly different, but you could tell they were related by looking at them.

I was the outcast: not the Ugly Duckling, but undeniably different. My build is slight, almost boyish, with next to no curves. I have wavy hair, a terrible ginger colour often associated with carrots. My eyes are sometimes mud brown and other times moss green. They generally reflect my mood, which is confused at the best of times. For my entire life I assumed I resembled our father, but I can't remember his hair and I don't have any photographs.

"Hello, girls," Rose said as she placed her jacket on the back of her chair and motioned for the waitress to serve her. She took a quick look at me and shook her head in dismay. "Bad day, Sweetie?"

"Just a little accident. I slipped."

"I would have gone home to change. Although, with the frequency that you spill things, you might consider keeping a change of clothes in your car. Oh, right. I forgot. You don't drive. Do you have a basket or something on your bike?"

"Nice to see you too, Rose." I stood and gave my sister a kiss on the cheek. Rose wrinkled her nose and resisted the urge to wipe away the damp spot, lest she smudge her make-up more. Sometimes I wonder if she has a split personality. Rose on her own can be quite sweet, but put in her a public place with the rest of our sisters and she turns into some kind of controlling creature.

"I see Iris and Lily are late. If you set a time to meet someone, you should be respectful enough to honour that time, don't you think?"

I refrained from pointing out that Rose was also late as the waitress appeared to take Rose's order.

"I'll have a café mocha, with skim milk, frothed, a little cinnamon sprinkled on top, and half caffeine, please." Rose dismissed the waitress with a little wave and turned her attention back to us. I'm always amazed that she never has to wait for anything. Daisy and I had sat for ten minutes before deciding to go to the counter to order our drinks ourselves. Rose simply sat and the waitress materialized.

"Of course, Lily was probably filthy from puttering around in her little garden and needed to take a shower. No doubt Iris is waiting on her at the train station since she won't drive into the city like a normal person."

Lily chose that moment to enter the shop, followed closely by Iris. "Sorry we're late. I had a little trouble at the greenhouse. One of my sprinklers was clogged so the gardenias weren't getting enough water. Tricky flowers, those ones. Anyway, long story short, I had to catch a later train than planned."

Lily pulled up a chair from another table and plopped herself into it. I could see Rose studying her grimy fingernails while trying to suppress a shudder. Undoubtedly, Rose would be taking Lily for a much needed manicure while she was in the city.

Before Iris had a chance to get settled, Rose pounced on our oldest sister. "Well, what's the big news?"

Patiently, Iris removed her sweater and settled herself into her chair. She placed her purse on the floor beside her and looked at each of us warmly.

Money, Masks & Madness

"Well?" Lily was getting antsy now. "You didn't even give me a hint on our way over here."

"I'm glad you were all able to make it." Iris looked up as the waitress came with Rose's order and asked for a coffee, no cream, no sugar.

"Well?" Daisy's usual patience started to diminish as the minutes ticked by and Iris continued to be silent.

"I just. Well. Oh—I may as well tell you straight out." She fiddled with the edge of her shirt, twisting it so tight, little lines appeared in the fabric. "I've been searching for Dad with the help of Travis. We think we might have found him."

I thought back to that day, long ago, when our mother decided we needed to desert our little paradise in the country. We hadn't heard from our father in months. It wasn't unusual for several weeks at a time to go by without hearing from him, but this was the longest he had ever disappeared from our lives. As children, we never questioned his absences. Admittedly, we didn't have anything to compare our family life to, so we never thought anything of the time he spent away from us. Now that I think about it, I can imagine what our mother must have thought.

She had always told us Daddy was at the market, selling his special herbs and spices that were grown especially in the forest. He usually worked hard throughout the spring and summer, tending to his fields—which were actually oversized gardens—often taking Lily and showing her which plants needed what type of care. As vegetables and flowers matured, he would harvest them and take them to the market, but usually returning within a few days.

His longer absences occurred closer to winter. After harvesting the herbs, he would tie them in bunches and hang them to dry in a special building he had constructed for that purpose. He would check the plants daily, always watching their progress and hoping for a good crop. Some years the yield was better than others, and other years the quality was better even though the quantity was lacking. Regardless of the outcome, he would weigh his produce, package it up carefully into small bundles and make the trip into the city.

He had told us it was a different kind of market than the vegetable and flower one, and that it took much longer to negotiate deals to make sure his wares ended up with the right people. We didn't think to question the process; we were too young to realize something strange was going on. Our mother never said anything about it. She made sure he had clean clothes and her wish list of items to purchase before sending him on his way with a kiss and a fleeting look of sadness.

As an adult, I can assume his activities were illegal. However, at the time we needed the money in order to maintain our privileged existence. We did plant a garden and ate a lot of what we grew. At the end of the season we would spend time together canning and freezing items for the winter. We kept a few chickens for eggs, a goat that produced milk and occasionally we would visit a local goat farm that made their own wonderful cheeses. Our mother was quite adept at sewing and without a television to occupy us, we all learned to keep busy with various chores, hobbies, and activities, not realizing these were all things that kept our living costs to a minimum. We never went without anything, but our parents were frugal as they never knew, from one year to the next, what profit their little hobby farm would bring in. In our eyes, the non-essentials were as plentiful as food had been. Our mom insisted she needed books, as much for teaching us how to read, as for her own entertainment. We each had at least one doll and board games which we treasured as they were often the only entertainment during long winter days when it was simply too cold to be outside for long. Our dad had given us the best life he could—or so we had been told.

His disappearance had saddened our mother like nothing else. After the first couple of months, she started to sit by the door, waiting for him to come home. She created delicious suppers, made sure the house was clean, and everything was ready for his homecoming. When four months had passed, she became determined to stick to routine, to show him she could survive without him and his treats from civilization. At the six month mark, our mother, who had always been busy and resourceful, became listless and unmotivated. Iris took on the homeschooling for Rose, Lily, and me, and Daisy took control of the household chores. In our hearts, we still held the hope that he would return, but in our minds, we knew it wasn't likely.

When a full year had passed, with no word or sign from him, my mother decided to pack up our meagre possessions and head back to civilization. We didn't own a car, or a phone, so for nearly twelve months we had had little to no contact with the outside world. It seemed like we walked for days, even though we were out of the forest by mid-afternoon and following a paved road into a small town. All this time we had been so close to people, real houses, and even a proper school. Our parents were aware of this, but as children, we hadn't known.

"It's probably another hour's walk to my parents' house." Our mother looked exhausted but we knew how determined she could be.

Always obedient, we trudged along behind her; Iris holding my hand so I wouldn't fall behind and Daisy prodding Lily to stay out of the puddles so we would look decent upon arrival at our grandparents' house.

What our mother hadn't told us was that she hadn't spoken to her mother in approximately ten years. When she had first moved out to our little wooden cabin, after the arrival of Iris, her mother would, on occasion, make a trip into the forest. She would drive her little car along the rutted excuse for a road, bearing luxuries such as store-bought soaps, diaper creams and other things to make raising a small child a bit easier. With each visit, she would also plead with her daughter to come home and raise her children in civilization.

As the paved road became littered with houses, our mother became increasingly nervous. She stopped abruptly at a street corner and turned to look at the five of us. As usual, Rose was impeccable; even the long walk hadn't ruffled her feathers. Mom tugged on my dress, shaking her head at its awkward fit. None of my sisters' hand-me-downs fit me properly, I was simply too skinny. After deeming Iris and Daisy somewhat presentable, Mom took in Lily.

Now here was a problem. Despite Daisy's best efforts, she hadn't been able to keep Lily out of the dirt. Her shoes were caked in mud, there was a dark smear across her cheek, and her curls had started to escape their braids. Determined, our mother spit into a rag of a handkerchief and scrubbed at Lily's face while Daisy took the initiative to smooth out the wayward braids.

"You'll have to do, I guess." Her voice sounded strange to me. I was seven, and couldn't quite put my finger on it, but I knew something was deeply disturbing my mom.

Iris lightly touched our mom's shoulder and smiled. "Whatever happens, it'll be ok. We'll make it work."

My mother seemed to take strength from Iris's support. She took a deep breath, handed her suitcase to Iris, took mine and Lily's hands (probably so Lily couldn't get dirty again), and marched up the walkway of a red brick house. It wasn't any bigger than our cabin in the woods, but something about it held an aura of elegance none of us had ever seen before. Perhaps it was because the house was encased in a lovely rust coloured brick with green shingles glinting in the sunshine. The rose bushes along the edges of the property were in bloom along with other varieties of flowers. Unlike our garden at home, this one was well-tended, without a weed in sight.

Mom dropped Lily's hand, straightened her own shirt, ran a damp palm over her blond hair, as though trying to smooth it and raised her hand to push a little button beside the door. At the time, I couldn't figure out why she didn't knock on the door. How on earth could the people inside know we were there?

After a few minutes, an elderly woman answered the door. If she hadn't looked so much like my mother, she might have frightened me for I had never seen someone with white hair and so many wrinkles. She looked like one of those apple dolls Daisy had tried to make for us the previous fall.

"Jane?" The one word came out in a gust of hope. "Is that really you?"

The old woman opened the screen door and stepped onto her front porch. My older sisters were lucky enough to be standing on the sidewalk below, but Lily and I were up close up with our mother, held firmly in place by what felt like a vice grip. As an adult, I now know she was clutching us for courage.

"Hi Mom." For the first time I could remember, my mother seemed to be a shadow of herself. "I would have called... but . . ."

My grandmother shook her head and ushered us inside her house. It was immaculate and I was afraid to step anywhere lest I make a mess. Lily wasn't so bothered by her surroundings. She sauntered inside, trailing bits of muck behind her.

"Take off your shoes, Lily," our mother instructed. Lily looked confused, but did as she was told. We always wore shoes in our house because the floors were so cold. The floor here was covered in some sort of beige fluffy fabric, not quite wool, but I didn't have a name for it. I followed the instructions given to Lily, as did my older sisters who were waiting outside the door.

"Well, you must be starving after such a long walk. Come into the kitchen and I'll see what I can find. If I'd known you were coming, I would have put on a nice roast of beef."

Never having had a roast of beef, I had no idea she meant she would have had us consume a living beast.

Money, Masks & Madness

My mom gave a little shudder but offered a small smile in response, while her own mother puttered around the kitchen, making little cheese and cucumber sandwiches, and filling glasses with the thinnest, strangest tasting milk I had ever consumed.

"We need to get some meat on these girls. Why, they're all skin and bones!" She was looking at me in particular. I glanced down at my loose fitting dress and shrugged my shoulders. It seemed I was always growing out of clothes before I actually grew into them.

And that was that. We were absorbed into her house, as though we had always belonged there.

Jennifer Bogart

Chapter Six

I brought my attention back to the present, where my sisters were squabbling over how Iris and Travis had managed to track down our father. For the past fourteen years our mother had been searching for him, but without any success.

"You still didn't tell us where he is," Rose pointed out. Her coffee had grown cold and she wrinkled her nose in distaste, refusing to drink the lukewarm brew.

Iris grimaced. "Well, you're not going to like it."

"Is he hurt, sick, mentally ill?" Daisy asked. "Whatever it is, we'll deal with it. Mom will be so excited to hear from him."

"I don't think she will be." Iris stared down at her coffee, biting her lip, and looking as though she wished the world would swallow her up. Maybe she was having second thoughts about sharing this news with us.

Lily gave her a gentle pat on the shoulder. "How bad can it be? Was he in jail all this time?"

Rose gasped, shocked her sister would propose such a thing, while Daisy looked equally horrified.

Iris smiled wryly. "That would be a much easier explanation as to where he's been all these years."

We looked from one to the other, trying to figure out what Iris wasn't saying to us. She could be secretive when she wanted to be. But if she didn't want us to know, she shouldn't have brought us all here to give us half the story.

"There's no point in holding back, you may as well tell us," I insisted, trying to keep my voice level and unemotional. Dealing with Iris was kind of like approaching a frightened animal. You had to be soft, steady and calm, otherwise she might bolt and we'd never discover her secrets.

"He was in jail, for a little bit." She looked around at each of us, her nervousness evident in the quietness of her voice. "The reason he didn't come home was because he had been selling illegal substances and finally got caught."

"I don't understand," Rose said. "We didn't have access to anything illegal. Just plants and herbs and all manner of organic stuff.

Lily snorted and it was clear she was trying to hold herself back from laughing outright at her older sister's naivety. "You really had no idea what special plants he was tending to for all those years? And why he chose to remain hidden in the forest? No postal address, no telephone, and no way to trace him?"

Rose and Daisy both shook their heads, looking baffled. After all this time in the city, I still couldn't believe how naive and innocent the two of them were. Rose really did see the world through the proverbial rose-coloured glasses. She was demanding and particular, but in all reality, she didn't see the ugliness in the world around her. Either that or she chose not to see it. Daisy liked to believe the very best of everyone. She had been hurt more than once because of her inability to see that there are people in the world who lie, cheat, and steal their way through life, regardless of who they might step on along the way.

"Are you two serious? Even Tulip knows better. Where have you been all these years?" Lily shook her head in disdain.

Gently, Iris placed a hand on her sister's shoulder. "They don't really need to know all the details, Lily."

"Yes they do," I interfered. "For that matter, so do I, and so does our mother. I honestly believe she thinks he's been dead all this time."

We all stared at Iris, waiting for her to explain our father's absence. It was Lily who supplied the details.

"His primary crop was high grade marijuana. He could easily grow it in the sunny patches of the forest, in quantities large enough to make a profit, but small enough not to get caught. He also cultivated mushrooms. Not the kind you eat in a salad or a stew, the kind that cause hallucinations. They were much easier to hide, but a bit trickier to grow."

"How do you know all this? How do we know you aren't making it all up?" Rose asked, her eyes narrowing.

Lily sighed and looked at each of us in turn. "I might have been nine when he disappeared, but by that point he had shown me how to care for his different plants and fungi, since the rest of you weren't terribly interested in the process. At the time, I didn't know what they were for, but it wasn't difficult to figure out as an adult."

Daisy actually had tears glistening in her cornflower blue eyes. "How could he?"

Lily shrugged her shoulders. "Fruits, vegetables, and wildflower posies don't quite bring in the kind of money we needed to be able to live the way we did."

"Is he still in jail?" I asked Iris. If he had been released, surely he would have come back to us, or at least tried to find us. We had lived with our grandmother for about a year after leaving the cabin. Once our mother had found steady employment, and was able to afford a house of her own, we had moved out and closer to the city.

Iris shook her head in response. "No. He was released."

"Well, when? Where is he?" Rose asked.

Daisy was studying her fingernails, trying to keep her tears under control. Iris looked away from us to stare at something out the window, her mind travelling away from the immediacy of the conversation.

"I'm not sure where he is now."

"But when was he released?" I asked quietly.

"About nine months after his incarceration. Three months before we moved in with grandma."

Anger bubbled up inside of me, threatening to spill over. Had he even bothered to try to find us?

"I think we should get a television." Chaz was buzzing around our little apartment, unable to stay still for long.

"Why? We're hardly ever here." My mind was still stuck on the conversation with my sisters. I seemed to be jammed in neutral.

He opened the fridge, took out some yogurt and started eating it directly from the container. I was glad to see it was the one full of sugary fruit, I wouldn't eat it anyway. But still, he could have had the decency to poor some into a bowl.

"For times like this when there's nothing to do."

I glanced up at the clock. "It's 7:00pm. There wouldn't be anything worth watching now anyway."

"Sure, we could get that PVR thing. Record all the stuff that's interesting and watch it when we're bored."

The problem with Chaz is that he's always bored. He'll look at a magazine for a total of five minutes before putting it down to find something else to occupy his mind. He might read a book for ten or fifteen minutes, but some distraction would call to him. I couldn't see him sitting through an hour long television show. Even a sitcom wasn't so likely to keep his attention.

As for me, I found the contrived characters, ridiculous plots, and unbelievable scenarios of television too much to bear. Real life has more to offer: real people, real issues, and real interactions. I would rather read a good book and play the scenes out in my head than have someone tell me specifically how something should look or a character should act.

Occasionally we would take in a movie, but each time we did, I generally ended up regretting the two hours of my life I could never get back. Aside from the extreme noise, flashing lights, and outlandish special effects; the stories never really came close to echoing the books. Not to mention Chaz's need to wander the theatre, returning every so often to get a quick update on what he missed before disappearing again to refill his popcorn. He's not the most attentive date.

"I don't think we need it."

I went back to reading my book, hoping to let it completely absorb me by the evolving conflict of the main characters. It was a sappy romance, completely unrealistic, but entertaining enough to hold my attention.

Chaz came to sit beside me on the arm of the couch. "Well, if I want a TV, there's really nothing stopping me."

"You're right. If you really want one, go get one. But don't expect me to pay for your cable bill. I already fork out for internet for the both of us," I replied, not taking my eyes from my book.

Gently, he touched my hair, forcing me to look up at him. "What's up, Buttercup? You don't seem yourself today."

I sighed and wished I could explain to him about my father. After all these years, I didn't think I should care so much. We had mourned him ages ago. In fact, he had officially been out of my life for longer than he had actually been in it. And even when he had been a part of it, he had hardly taken any notice of us, except for Lily. It was clear to all of us that the reason he paid her any attention at all was so she could propagate the family business—the very illegal family business.

"I'm fine. It was just a long week and now I'm tired."

I tried to return my attention to my book, but Chaz wouldn't have any of it. He started to massage my shoulders and I felt myself melt back into him. Like the rest of him, his fingers were long, lean, and strong. He seemed to know exactly where the knots were as he kneaded the muscles between my shoulder blades.

If only he were boyfriend material... but he wasn't. His relationships lasted about as long as his attention span for magazines did.

"We should go out. Get a change of scenery," he announced as I was starting to relax. "There's a pretty cool club that opened on Crescent Street a few weeks ago, I'd love to check it out. Paige and some of your coworkers will be there."

Money, Masks & Madness

Mentioning Paige wasn't the best way to convince me to go out. "I don't know. We always go out so late, and end up coming home so close to morning that we sleep away the next day. I'm tired tonight and want to relax. Maybe take a bubble bath and read for a bit."

Chaz's fingers were working their magic on my neck, shoulders, and upper back. I could feel myself starting to drift off to sleep. Periodically his fingers would make contact with skin and I resisted the little shivers that ran up my spine. "Why don't you skip the bath and take a good long nap. When you wake up, you'll be all refreshed and ready to go out. Don't worry; I won't let you oversleep so you miss all the fun."

Maybe if I really fell asleep, he would leave me be, and let me sleep through the night. No sooner did that thought enter my mind then reality shoved it out of the way. Chaz might seem like a flighty kind of guy, but once he got something in his head, there would be no changing his mind.

"Mmmm . . ." My mind didn't seem to want to form coherent words.

"See you're feeling better already." He gently slipped a pillow under my head and reached over to dim the lights as I drifted off into a comfortable sleep.

As I floated between wakefulness and a dream state, my mind wandered through all the different possibilities of why my father hadn't returned to us after serving his jail term. Perhaps he had been struck on the head and suffered amnesia, or worse, had been maimed in some way and had been afraid to come back to us, his own family.

Regardless, I was certain he would be thrilled to see us. Iris was in the process of tracking down his current address. Having a policeman as a husband certainly had its advantages. Travis was a super nice guy, too bad the rest of us haven't been able to find someone as sweet and charming as him.

I let go of my conscious state and let the inner workings of my brain take over, losing myself in the soft rhythm of the music Chaz had put on his iPod. I could worry about my dad later; after all, I hadn't bothered to worry about him for the past thirteen years, so why should it matter so much to me now?

Chapter Seven

"Are you wearing eyeliner?"

Chaz turned to glare at me; his bright blue eyes were clearly enhanced by the slightest edging of black. He already had thickly fringed lashes, so I couldn't fathom why he would wear make-up.

"I had a photo-shoot this afternoon and couldn't get all the make-up off." He returned his attention to the refrigerator, making it impossible for me to see his face.

"Liar. You weren't wearing it when I came home from work. I wasn't that tired, I would have noticed." After a three hour nap, followed by a shower, and something to eat, I was feeling energized and refreshed—ready to take on Montreal's night life. "Go wash your face. I'm not going out in public with you looking like that."

Chaz muttered something and slammed the fridge door shut. In one hand, he had an apple and in the other, he held a raw hot dog. "I'm the one who invited you out, remember?"

"I do and I'm not going if you insist on wearing that gunk on your face. You look ridiculous."

I looked directly at him and smiled, using my best imitation of Rose. We stood there, staring at each other, each determined to win. Being the youngest of five girls,

I think I had the upper hand in this battle of wills. I knew the moment I won. He started to fidget with the food in his hands and sighed audibly. Within seconds he looked away and shook his head.

"Fine."

I smiled as I watched him storm into the bathroom. Thank goodness for that. Chaz was a quirky one at the best of times. I really didn't mind his unique fashion sense. Occasionally he came home with piercings in unusual places but they only lasted a month or two at most. His hair colour he played with more, but part of his profession demanded flexibility in his appearance. Makeup was out of the question, as far as I was concerned. I'm not a prude and I rarely say anything about his choices, but men in eyeliner was a bit of an issue for me. Perhaps because I was immersed in fake visages all day long and I liked to see what lay beneath the paint.

When Chaz emerged from the bathroom, he looked more like the man I knew and loved, even if he was a little on the grumpy side. A faint outline remained along his lower lash line but I knew there wasn't anything that could be done about it.

"Much better." I nodded my approval.

I glanced at my watch. It was a few minutes after eleven, which meant the clubs would be starting to fill up now. We were supposed to be meeting up with some of Chaz's modeling and movie friends. An outgoing bunch that played as hard as they worked. Granted, for the most part, playing was a type of work for them because someone somewhere might see them, become interested, and magically another gig would appear out of what seemed to have been an innocent night of socializing.

Money, Masks & Madness

We met Chaz's gang of friends outside the new club he wanted to try. It was pretty much like every other dance club in Montreal: dark and dreary on the outside; hot, noisy, and disco-esque on the inside. As the lights flashed purple, red, and yellow, I surveyed the room, amazed at how people seemed to be able to carry on conversations despite the volume of the music. It was your standard mix of dance music, with seemingly endless songs and music created by anything but traditional instruments. I overheard one of Chaz's friends mention something about the singer being auto-tuned. I tried to figure out what he was talking about, but I couldn't hear the vocals over the heavy rhythm reverberating through the room.

Chaz handed me a drink before going in search of Paige. I vaguely wondered if she might be his newest crush and wished I had the heart to tell him she didn't seem overly interested in men. Well, at least as far as I could tell she wasn't. Of course, with all of Chaz's eccentricities, one could hardly classify him as your traditional man. He liked flamboyant colours, unusual fashion, and now his newest folly—the eye makeup. Suddenly, it dawned on me that perhaps he had wanted to wear to it to impress Paige. He couldn't be that silly about her, could he?

Luckily, I found her before he did.

"Heya, Paige," I shouted at her. She raised her drink at me and nodded in return.

"Chaz is looking for you."

Again she nodded in response and I began to wonder if she could actually hear me.

"I said," I yelled as loudly as I could, "Chaz has the biggest crush on you!"

Her response was the same and I began to giggle, secure in knowing she had no idea what I was saying. "In fact, he thinks you're the most fabulous girl he's ever met. Of course, he wants to meet Adam Green even more, so I'm not sure where that puts you in the grand scheme of things."

Another nod, accompanied by a vacant smile, which made me laugh more. Paige laughed too, and before we knew it, we were melting together in a puddle of giggles. One cranberry and vodka and I couldn't control myself.

Chaz found us, wiping tears from our eyes and still trying to control our laughter. He raised an eyebrow at me, but I ignored him. Somehow, he managed to wordlessly convince Paige to dance with him. I watched as the two of them did their version of dancing to the pulsating music. A bump here, a grind there, some shifting of the feet. They weren't graceful or athletic but they sure did look like they were having fun.

Somewhere inside of me, a little green gremlin poked her head up out of a pool of jealousy. The feeling took me by surprise and I couldn't seem to let it go. Chaz had invited me out tonight and here he was flirting with Paige while I was stuck at the bar by myself. I shook my head, trying to fling the evil gremlin far from my thoughts. I wanted Chaz to be happy; he should be off dancing with Paige.

"Can I get you a drink?"

I looked up to see Adam Green standing beside me. My mouth dropped open in shock. Although, when I thought about it, I shouldn't have been surprised to see him. Adam must have been the real reason Chaz was so keen to go out. Suddenly, the little green gremlin was back with mischief in her eyes.

"Uh, sure," I shouted back, trying to hide my shock under false bravado. Of course, another drink would probably have me dancing on tables, but I would sip it, and be no worse for wear come morning. It was still early, so I had plenty of time to nurse the drink.

Since I was already leaning against the bar, all he had to do was lean over me to place the order. Admittedly, I was a little unnerved by his proximity. I could smell his aftershave, something light but masculine as his arm brushed my shoulder and his cheek came close to my face. When he leaned back, I gave myself a little mental shake. Adam was a good-looking guy, there was no denying that, but surely he was so far out of my league I would need a jetpack to reach him.

"Are you here with friends?" he asked.

I nodded; surprised I could actually make out what he was saying to me. "Paige is here, from the studio, and my roommate, Chaz. He's dying to meet you."

I closed my eyes, mortified I had actually said that out loud. Chaz would kill me. It was one thing to fool around with Paige while I was certain she couldn't understand a word I was saying. It was another to talk to Adam Green about my roommate's desire to meet him. One look at Chaz and Adam might get the wrong impression.

Adam smiled, revealing a small dimple in his left cheek. I liked how his dark eyes twinkled under the strobe lights and had no trouble understanding why he might be considered the next up and coming actor in the Montreal film industry. Good looking, personable—and from the way his dress shirt pulled across his shoulders, I'm sure he had the body to match.

"Are you here with friends?" I asked, trying to cover up my blunder.

"I was supposed to meet my brother here, but I'm pretty sure he stood me up." Adam paid the bartender and handed me my drink. Since I hadn't told him what I wanted, I wasn't sure what I was drinking. I only knew it was strong, sweet, pink, and was definitely quenching my thirst. The club was now filled wall to wall with dancers, drinkers, and party-goers, so there was, quite literally, standing room only.

"I'm sorry to hear that." Alistair was so particular; I couldn't imagine him standing up his own brother. He demanded the best from everyone around him, but that was generally because that's what he gave out. Aside from the way he delivered his orders—that could use a little improvement—he was generally courteous and polite.

One shoulder lifted in a nonchalant shrug. "It's not a big deal. I have you to entertain me."

He winked at me and I wrinkled my nose, not quite sure how to respond to his flirting. Guys had flirted with me before. I'm not all that naive but I am a straight-forward kind of person. I don't play games. I prefer honesty up front, mostly because I can't always differentiate between genuine interest and playful but noncommittal flirting. That didn't mean I wouldn't take the time to get to know a person I found interesting. It just meant that I hated when someone leads you on but in the end has no real interest in you at all. It had happened too many times as a teenager. Some older boy would come along and make me feel all special and fuzzy inside when his real mission was to spend hours drooling over one of my older, blonder, more beautiful sisters.

I'm not ugly. I'm not even close to ugly—but not everyone is attracted to slim red heads with freckles, especially not teenage boys. The experience taught me to be a little wearier of men than I might have otherwise been.

"So, do you go clubbing a lot?" Adam asked as he started to lead me away from the busy bar area. This was probably a good thing. Alcohol and I don't always mix so well.

"Oh, you know if there's nothing better to do on a Thursday, Friday, or Saturday night." Now why had I said that? I did, occasionally go to the bar, but not every weekend. Well, not every night of every weekend, unless Chaz needed a date or had a show of some sort. I had a life outside of work and partying.

"You don't seem the type to me."

"Huh?" What was that supposed to mean? "Why do you say that?"

"Well, you gave me the impression that you're a wheatgrass and organics kind of girl. I can picture you digging in a garden or hiking through a forest. Dancing in a club, I'm not so sure about."

"Really? I love dancing." This was the truth, I did love dancing. And I love music, in small bunches, usually something a little less pulsating with lyrics that actually made sense. Perhaps I was born in the wrong era, or perhaps it was my mother's influence—she was, after all, a child of the seventies.

He took the now empty glass from my hand, replaced it with his own hand, and pulled me onto the crowded dance floor. There was so little room to move, the best anyone could really do was sway with the music, maybe wriggle your hips a bit. This wasn't real dancing, the kind that gets your heart rate up and your blood moving. This was for people who were too cool to move. Noticing a small open area of floor out of the corner of my eye, I shimmied in that direction. Adam could stay or follow, it really didn't matter to me. If I could reach that little square, I would claim it for myself, and show him and everyone else what dancing was really all about.

Chapter Eight

Of course, he followed, all the while smiling and watching. Laughing, I threw my head back, letting my red curls fall free down my back, and luxuriating in the bit of space I found to move. As the music continued to pulse around me, I lost focus on whom and where I was, and let the beat take me away. I didn't care that Adam was watching or my actions were probably less than graceful. All I cared about was the music entering my soul and propelling me to express its beauty through movement.

As I started spinning in circles, my feet moving faster and faster in an attempt to keep up with the music, the room also started to spin. Much to my dismay, I tripped over my own two feet and would have landed on my butt if Chaz hadn't grabbed me around the waist before I hit the ground. Adam was laughing hysterically.

"Oh, Chaz," I said, my breath coming in small gasps. "You saved me."

Gently, he made sure I was securely on my feet before deciding to wrap an arm around my waist to keep me steady. The look on his face didn't mirror his actions at all.

"Is that how you treat a lady?" Chaz demanded of Adam. "Get her drunk and let her make a complete fool of herself in public? You didn't even try to keep her from falling. She could have hurt herself."

Chaz angry is really something to see. His slight accent increases, his blue eyes narrow and start to shoot little slivers of ice, and his chest puffs out, all masculine muscle.

Adam looked from Chaz to me, perplexed. "Are you her boyfriend?"

"No," I said, but it came out as a slur, and I'm fairly certain Adam didn't hear it.

"I'm her friend, that's all the likes of you needs to know." Chaz was ready to turn around and leave Adam, but Paige was blocking his way.

"Oh, I see you've met Adam," she said to Chaz. "Is he all that you hoped he would be?"

A look of confusion crossed Chaz's features. Even in my hazy state, I knew what Paige was referring to. How on earth had she heard me earlier? Mortified, I tried to twist away from Chaz, but he held me firm.

"This is Adam Green?"

Paige nodded, her green eyes glinting with mischief. "Tulip told me you practically idolize him. Well, next to me that is."

I wished the dance floor would suddenly develop a sinkhole and swallow me up. Montreal was notorious for sinkholes, but unfortunately I didn't have the wherewithal to make one appear. In my next life, I wanted to come back as a witch or a wizard or even a sorcerer. I didn't care, as long as it was something—anything—with magical powers.

"You told Paige I idolize her?" Chaz asked. Rather than turn his frosty gaze on me, his eyes looked sad and disappointed. As foggy as my brain felt, even I knew I had done something terribly wrong.

He was my best friend and I had treated him poorly so I could have a little laugh all to myself. I felt my bottom lip begin to quiver and sniffed, trying to hold back tears. I never meant to hurt Chaz. As much as he drove me crazy, he would never have done something like that to me.

"No." I was telling the truth. The word idolize had never left my lips. "Plus, I told her you like Adam more than you like her." I clamped my hand over my mouth before anymore words could escape.

Chaz dropped his arm from my shoulder, glared at me, and stormed away.

I tried to copy his expression, but I'm pretty sure I made a muddled mess out of it. When I turned back towards him, all I could see was his purple clad shoulders making their way through the crowd towards the exit. All that was left for me to do was to follow him and hope he would forgive me.

On the street, the night air was cool and humid. The sidewalk looked as though it had rained while we were inside. Not a downpour, just a little drizzle that chased away the worst of the day's heat. Chaz was leaning against the corner of the building, a lit cigarette held in one hand.

"Chaz?"

Lightly, I touched his shoulder, hoping he wasn't too angry with me. He kept his face hidden from my view, and his body began to tremble. Could he be crying? Was it possible I had injured his pride that badly?

"I'm so sorry. I don't know what came over me." Taking a deep breath, I prepared to launch into a speech about what a horrible friend I was. "I honestly didn't think she could hear me over the music. Every time I said something, she nodded and agreed with me. I'm so sorry. I would never, ever –"

When he turned around I could see his shoulders were shaking with laughter.

"Are you laughing at me? Do you think this is funny? I thought you were out here hating me! Maybe even thinking about making phone calls to find a new place to live."

I folded my arms across my chest and leaned against the rough brick of the building. Even though I knew my reaction was childish, I couldn't stop my features from sliding into a pout, complete with my bottom lip sticking out. The two of us stood there for ages, neither one of us willing to break the angry silence. Although he might have found the situation amusing on some level, he was obviously annoyed.

"Oh, Tulip, you did it to yourself."

Chaz turned towards me. Since his face was half hidden in the shadows of the street lamp, I couldn't see his expression. His body was still, the laughter completely gone.

I had no response for him. Anything I did say in defence would be construed as excuses; there was nothing I could offer to justify my actions. He had spoken to me in confidence, let me know things about him he would never share with anyone else, and I had treated it like a joke.

"I'm sorry," I whispered. "I wish I could take it back." One tear slowly rolled down my cheek, hastily I brushed it away. I didn't have the right to cry, I had created this mess myself.

"I know." His simple words made the tears fall even faster. In all my life, I think Chaz is the only person to have had the privilege to see me cry. "Come here, Buttercup."

He pulled me into his arms, enveloping me in security and warmth. Trust Chaz to be the one comforting me when I was the one who had hurt him.

"You always do stupid things when you drink." His hand was gently rubbing my back. I nodded against his chest, knowing he was right. "That's why I came looking for you. You drank the first vodka and cranberry so fast, and I saw you accept the second drink from that idiot. You know better than that."

"I know. You're right." I sniffed, took a deep breath and leaned back in his arms. The night air was cool, but Chaz enveloped me in comforting warmth. "You're one of the good guys, Chaz Selinzky."

"I know."

I laughed at his easy confidence and gave him a playful pat. "Do you want to go back in?"

He shook his head, continuing to hold me close. "Not particularly. Let's go find something scrumptious for dessert. I've seen enough bitterness tonight and could use something sweet."

I wasn't quite sure I understood what he was talking about, but I let him take my hand and lead me away from the club.

As per my usual routine Monday morning, I woke early, brewed myself a cup of organic tea and switched on my laptop. I made a habit of checking it before going to work because both Iris and Rose had a tendency to send me messages via email rather than pick up the phone to call.

Poor Mrs. Akiss had sent me three messages over the weekend. She must have thought I had forgotten about her. Well, to be honest, I sort of had, although not on purpose. Somehow, between Iris's revelation on Friday night and my slight hangover on Sunday morning, I managed to forget all about Mrs. Akiss and her terrible plight. Chaz spent his Sunday at one of the various festivals while I nursed my headache and slept most of the day away.

Setting my tea aside, I gave my full attention to Mrs. Akiss's emails. In each one she was increasingly agitated; worried about her child, his safety, her health, and her nefarious family getting their hands on her husband's hard earned wealth. She was grateful I was interested in helping her with her own health, but she doubted she would live to make the long trek across the ocean. Her primary concern remained her son.

This woman was so selfless when it came to her child, I wondered if I would be the same if I ever had children. My own mother would have and, in fact, did do everything in her power to keep us safe.

In our younger years she kept us from the influences of the modern world in an attempt to raise children who were uncorrupted by materialism. When it was apparent she would be left to fend for herself and raise the five of us in the wilderness, she took it upon herself to find a solution she could live with.

Along with our few meagre possessions, she packed up her pride and trudged the kilometres to her parents' house. As an adult, I now know what it took for her to ask her mother for help. We were lucky we had a grandmother with an open heart. As often as our grandmother criticized our mother for keeping her grandbabies secluded and raising us like barbarians (which was far from the truth—our manners are impeccable, except for Lily), she also praised her on her strength and determination.

I hesitated briefly before typing my reply. More than anything, I wanted to help this woman, but at the same time, I needed to make sure she was for real.

Dear Mrs. Akiss,

I can imagine the pain and suffering you are feeling right now. In addition to your physical pain, your heart is undoubtedly breaking for your child. I know if I had children of my own, I would do whatever it took to protect them from all the evils in the world.

I am anxious to meet your young son. Could you please send me a picture of him? I have attached a picture of myself so you may see you are truly dealing with a young, honest woman, and not someone who is trying to swindle you out of your husband's fortune.

Kindest Regards,

Tulip

I scanned the message for mistakes and proceeded to search through the few digital photos I had, looking for the perfect one to attach to the message. Most of these pictures had been taken by Chaz, as I didn't even own a regular camera. He liked to take pictures almost as much as he liked to have his picture taken. I found one I liked of me, at the Botanical Gardens, next to the gardenias.

They were in full bloom and looked absolutely gorgeous. I was wearing a simple pink sundress, and my red hair was pulled off my face with butterfly barrettes. Chaz had teased me about those barrettes, telling me they made me look like a twelve year old. I wore them anyway, just as he had worn the bright yellow, skin tight satin shorts I thought were hideous.

No sooner had I sent the message off then Chaz came out his room. Another early morning for him on a weekday? He must have another audition or something.

"Want waffles?" he asked me, as he started to pull the ingredients out of the fridge.

"You offering?" I knew he wasn't, but it didn't hurt to ask. Maybe one of these days he would surprise me.

His laughter filled our tiny apartment. I was so relieved our little tiff from Saturday night had been forgiven already. Neither one of us were much for holding grudges, probably because we loved each other too much to stay angry for long.

"I didn't think so," I said as I shut down my laptop and made my way over to our little kitchen table. There was nothing like starting the day off right.

Chapter Nine

"You're going to be the death of me, Tulip," Alistair said as I handed him a less than perfect coffee.

I rolled my eyes at him and tried to keep my comments to myself. At least he was remembering my name today. If he wanted his coffee a specific way, he should either make it himself or purchase a newer machine that actually did what it was supposed to.

I'm not sure what was different about today, but instead of handing the cup back to me, he took it and turned away. I stood there, staring after him, the shock evident on my face.

He turned back, smiled and asked, "Well, are you coming?"

Startled by his reaction, I took a moment before realizing I needed to make my feet move.

Nothing about Alistair was right this morning; he was a little softer around those rough edges, his smile came easily, and the compliments were plentiful. This was a side of him I hadn't seen before and I briefly began to wonder if perhaps someone had put something in his cereal this morning. I knew the coffee hadn't been spiked.

"See how the skin tone is a bit greyer on this side? You need to lighten it up a bit and let some of the pink shine through. He's supposed to be undead, not completely decayed."

I watched him as he gave Derek instructions on how to improve his mask so he wouldn't have to dismantle it completely. With the deadline coming up in a few weeks, I couldn't believe how calm Alistair was. If it were my career on the line, I think I would be in all-out panic mode, considering all that still needed to be done.

He watched Paige as she carefully glued individual strands of rust-coloured hair to her mask. I could barely stand to look at the thing but forced myself to give her my full attention. The last thing I wanted was for her to think I was too embarrassed to look her in the eye after the weekend's debacle.

"Paige, darling, you need to relax and take your time. You're so close to finishing but you're starting to look like you might be rushing things a bit."

Alistair gently pulled a clump of hair away from the mask, luckily it hadn't dried yet. Normally the hair would be sewn into the mask, but for some reason, they had opted to use adhesive instead. Paige pursed her lips and carefully took one strand of hair with a pair of tweezers. Gently, she placed it on the zombie's skull and pressed it into place. Alistair nodded his approval before moving on. As we walked past her station, I took a quick glance back, but she didn't look up from her work. Either she was really angry with me or she was equally embarrassed. I would have to wait until lunch to find out.

By lunchtime, Alistair had exhausted me with his niceness. His sweet temperament, polite suggestions, and helpful hints were beginning to drive me insane. I wanted the old crotchety Alistair back: the one who made me brew four cups of coffee until I got it right, the one who called me anything but my name, and the one who made his staff run in fear of the possibility of having to start from scratch again. At the very least, that Alistair had been entertaining and honest. He made the hours fly by. The new and not so improved Alistair was boring. I felt like I was in some horrible time warp, where the minutes on the clock last for hundreds of seconds instead of sixty. I wasn't sure how much more I could take.

"Sweetheart, will you run this over to Gerald for me? I want to make sure I have the right colour palette."

It took me a minute to realize he was talking to me. So, now he was calling me by endearments? Terrific.

"I'm not carrying that thing through the streets of Montreal," I said to him.

He was holding out a Styrofoam head with Paige's fresh zombie masks fitted over it. At first glance, people would think I was carrying a rotting head under my arm. While in theory, that might sound like a hilarious prank, I knew it was a recipe for disaster.

"I didn't mean for you to carry it around for the world to see." He chuckled and shook his head. "In the storeroom you'll find a carrying case for it. I would hate for anything to happen to this masterpiece en route."

"Right. Of course." Gingerly, I took the head from him, trying to touch it as little as possible. The latex had the rubbery feel of old vegetables and smelled equally bad. To my unpracticed eye, it wasn't one of their better masks, but I wasn't about to argue with him.

Once I had the head safely concealed in the carrier, I made my way into the street, feeling a little conspicuous by the bold advertising on the case. Alistair couldn't keep the contents of the box completely secret because that wasn't his style. Instead, the case was covered in a custom design featuring his most colourful creations along with the company logo, website, and phone number. So now, any would-be stalkers would be able to track me down, too. Not that I expected it to be an issue, but I had heard stories.

One of the problems with Montreal is that it's an old city. Parts of it look all modern, but others are difficult to manipulate with cobblestones and holes in the pavement. Like all cities, wherever you go in the summer, you'll be redirected because of construction. I tripped along the sidewalk, listening to a tune playing itself in my mind and enjoying the walk on such a gorgeous summer day, far too preoccupied to take note of the uneven ground beneath my high heeled sandals. The sudden dip in the sidewalk took me by surprise and before I knew it, I was sprawled on the ground with my skirt flipped up around my hips. Mortified, I pulled it down with a jerk, picked myself up, and reached over to retrieve the case. Thankfully, it had done its job and protected the precious cargo inside. As I grasped the handle and started to pick it up, the latch popped open and the head rolled out.

Within seconds a woman started screaming hysterically. Another grabbed her small child, covered his eyes, and took off at a run. At least half a dozen people whipped out their cell phones, no doubt calling the police to protect them from a five foot nothing, 100 pound monster in a sundress. Alistair was going to kill me.

"It's ok," I called to the throng of people who began to mill around. "It's a prop. Nothing to worry about."

Hastily, I stuffed the head back into the case, not caring what kind of damage it may have sustained. As I closed it, I noticed a few strands of hair catch in the latch, along with bits of rubbery skin, so I opened it back up, amid horrified gasps, and pushed it all back in. All the while, I was thinking I could kiss this job good-bye. It might not have been my dream job but it was better than being a dog walker.

Just as I was certain I had everything under control, and the crowd was beginning to disperse, a police officer approached me. He looked like he had drunk one too many cups of coffee this morning. His shaking right hand hovered over his gun and he held his left up in front him, fingers splayed, as though he were trying to ward off some kind of evil force. Did I really look that menacing?

"Put the case down, ma'am and place your hands on your head." He seemed to be making a great effort to keep his tone neutral but firm. He was failing miserably, as I detected a slight tremor.

"It's a mask; it's not real," I said, but dutifully set down the case.

For some reason, the latch didn't want to stay shut. The moment the case hit the pavement, it popped open again. When I looked inside at the gory mess, even I had a hard time believing it was completely innocent. Slowly, I stood, pushed the case towards him with my toe, and placed my hands on my head.

From behind me, another officer grabbed me and before I knew it, my wrists were handcuffed behind my back. I sighed in frustration but knew better than to say or do anything. Lucky for me, he hadn't tried to wrestle me to the ground. I guess I didn't look all that menacing after all.

The officer in front of me practically tiptoed his way over to the case. Had the situation not been so serious, I probably would have succumbed to the giggles. First he pushed the case with his toe and then he bent forward to give the contents a closer inspection. He couldn't possibly believe the thing was real. The look of disgust on his young features had me choking back giggles at the absurdity of the situation. The officer behind me gave my arm a little shake and I managed to regain control. I knew the moment the nervous one decided the mask wasn't real or harmful; his entire body relaxed with a visible sigh.

"Is this a practical joke?" he asked me. I think he was trying to regain his composure in front of the crowd that had gathered.

"No sir," I responded, shaking my head vehemently. "I work for Alistair Green, at the Macabre Mercantile. This is one of his pieces. Well, not one of his pieces. He's fully intact. And it's not one he created; he would never send one of those out for validation. I'm pretty sure it belongs to Paige, I could be wrong though, it's hard to tell now. But it's from his shop which is a few blocks away."

He studied the mask with such intensity I wondered what nonsense would spill from his mouth next. "Was this some kind of publicity stunt?"

I shook my head again. "No. I tripped, on the hole in the sidewalk." If my hands had been free, I would have pointed at it. All I could do was nod in the general direction I had come from.

He looked from me to the case, as though weighing his words carefully. "Let her go, we can't hold her."

Within seconds I felt the jiggle of the handcuffs as the officer worked the tiny key in the lock. As they fell away, I became aware of how uncomfortable I had been while standing there. I was glad I wasn't in those things any longer. If I had been, I probably would have lost feeling in my arms. As it was, the distinct sensation of pins and needles was working its way from wrist to elbow. I wanted to shake out my arms to get the blood flowing, but I worried the officers might think I was going to hit them or something.

I didn't lose any time in bending down to close the case, making sure all parts and pieces of the mask were contained inside. Carefully, I took the time to secure the latch, double checking it to make sure it was locked tight.

"I'm free to go?" I asked because I didn't want to take the chance of being tackled to the ground.

The younger officer nodded. "Just try to keep that thing contained."

"Right."

With more confidence than I was feeling, I marched through the crowd that looked less shocked and seemed to be busy snapping pictures and filming video. I could imagine where all those images were going to turn up. Alistair was going to have the biggest hissy fit ever.

Jennifer Bogart

Chapter Ten

As soon as the door slammed shut behind me, Alistair appeared to engulf me in a huge bear hug. His aftershave reminded me of the woods, slightly floral, a little musky, and refreshing compared to some of the more cloying scents Chaz sometimes favoured. Not sure how to react, I stood there, waiting for him to let go of me.

"You're a star!" He pushed away long enough to shout these words in my face and hugged me close again. Something strange was definitely going on here.

"You really are," Paige commented dryly. She wasn't at her workstation finishing her latest piece for the movie. Instead, she was sitting in front of the computer. Unfortunately, she was blocking the screen from my view.

"I don't understand."

"News travels fast in the industry, thanks to handy tools like Google Alerts and smartphones. When the first video was posted on YouTube, I thought it was just a coincidence. When the second popped up, I figured I should take a look."

Alistair had finally let go of me and was now motioning for Paige to pull up the video in question. "Now, the quality isn't great, but we can clearly see our name on the case and the mask on the ground."

He clicked on the arrow to play the video and I had the privilege of reliving my embarrassment in front of my coworkers. It was one thing to have suffered through that episode without their knowledge and quite another to see the entire ordeal on a screen for millions of people to see.

Already I could see that hundreds had viewed it and several had made comments. Alistair should have been horribly angry over the destruction of one of his prized masks, but instead he was delighted with the publicity. He even howled with laughter as he watched the officer approach the mask with extreme caution.

I looked awful on screen. My dress was filthy from where I had fallen on the ground, there was a scuff of dirt across my left cheek, and my hair was a tangled mess. In fact, I looked like a hysterical actress from one of Alistair's horror movies before being attacked in a dark and deserted building. I sincerely hoped my sisters and Chaz didn't get a look at this. I was about to excuse myself so I could get cleaned up in the bathroom when Alistair started to play the next video in the queue, this one was taken from a different angle. When I looked to the right sidebar, I could see video after video, of varying quality, showcasing my folly.

"Alistair, I'm so sorry about the mask." Horrified, I looked away, trying to keep my tears of embarrassment from falling.

"Who cares about the mask? This exposure is worth a thousand masks. We haven't checked out Facebook yet, but I'm pretty sure the pictures and videos will go viral there in no time."

"Great," I muttered and turned away. I didn't need to see all the different versions, I had already lived it. I couldn't believe how horrible our society was. Instead of stopping to see if I was okay, or calling the police because they believed there really was a rotting body part in that case (as I had originally thought), the passersby had simply taken out their various cell phones, iPods, and other electronic devices to record the event.

Nice.

It was a good thing this hadn't been a serious incident. I couldn't imagine how these people would have reacted if the head inside had been real and not a cheap latex imitation. Then again, after seeing and living it first hand—I think I already knew the answer. We are so desensitized by technology that we don't stop to think about what is right and what is wrong. We get so caught up in the moment of shock value that we forget we aren't actually living in a movie at all.

Shaking my head in disgust, I made my way to the bathroom, cleaned up, and grabbed my purse. It was five o'clock and I was done for the day. As I let myself out of the building, I could hear the laughter of my coworkers, caught up in the same wave of technology wonder.

Remembering I had hung my laundry outside to dry before heading off to work, I went straight to the backyard to remove it from the line. I had only hung up about six pairs of underwear along with matching bras, so I didn't need to make the trip upstairs to collect a clothes basket. When I entered the yard, I stared at the naked line in confusion. They were gone. All of them. Now what was I going to wear tomorrow?

I marched up the stairs, hoping Chaz had done me a favour and removed them before the other tenants complained I had left them out all day. The little circular line was for everyone's use, but we did have to be respectful and remove things promptly.

"Chaz? Did you collect my laundry from the line for me?" I asked as I shoved open the door.

He was sitting on the couch with a rather large box in front of him. "Huh?"

"My laundry. I hung it up this morning on my way to work and it's not there. Did you bring it up?"

"Nope. Maybe check with one of our neighbours." He turned his attention back to the contents of the box. Sighing, I left the apartment, not bothering to shut the door. I needed to find my underwear.

After knocking on the other three doors in our building and being rudely told to go away, I began to panic. I couldn't afford to go out and replace all those sets. And I certainly didn't have time to do it tonight. I would have to wash what I was wearing today and hope it dried overnight.

"Any luck?" Chaz asked. The box had disappeared and in its place was a brand new flat screen TV. It was pretty small, but it didn't look right, sitting in the middle of our coffee table.

"What's that?" I asked. I wasn't paying for cable or satellite or anything like that—not when I had to go out and buy all new underwear.

"This?" He looked at the television as though contemplating what it could possibly be doing in the middle of our apartment. "It's a TV. You've seen a TV before, Tulip."

"Of course I know it's a TV! What's it doing here? I thought we discussed this and we weren't going to get one."

He looked up at me for a few seconds before answering quietly. "If I remember correctly, you discussed it; I listened and went out and bought it."

"I can't afford that right now! I have to buy new underwear. Bras are expensive. And I know you know. I've seen you looking in magazines." I sat down on the couch beside him, still muttering under my breath even though I knew he wasn't listening.

I picked up the phone, it was an old rotary handset and I loved the rattling noise it made while each number pulsed its way through the myriad of wires. We had a wireless somewhere in the apartment, but I never seemed to be able to find it.

"Who are you calling?"

"The police," I answered absently. "I need to report a robbery."

He laughed softly and returned his attention to his newest prize. It seemed he had also bought a DVD player. I began to wonder if he won the lottery or something. He pretended to fiddle with some wires while eavesdropping on my conversation. With the way my day was going, no doubt I was more entertainment than anything you could watch in a box.

I have to admit, the police were patient and kind, but it seemed they were holding back laughter, thinking this was some kind of joke.

"Could you describe the missing articles, ma'am?" The man at the other end of the phone started out, sounding bored.

"Yes. Six sets of underwear. They're all different colours, but they match. One is pale blue, with satin ribbon trim, one is pink with lace ruffles and little bows, another—"

What sounded like a cough interrupted me and I paused.

"Would this... uh... underwear be thongs, bikinis or granny panties?"

"A mix of styles, but no granny panties," I replied. I would save those for when I was older. "One set is boy shorts, yellow with little white polka—"

Another strangled sound came through the phone wires, interrupting my list.

"Is something wrong?" I asked.

After much throat clearing and what sounded suspiciously like smothered chuckles, the officer on the other end responded. "Is this some kind of joke?"

"No. I hung my laundry out to dry this morning. When I returned home from work, it was missing. I checked with the neighbours and they haven't seen or heard anything out of the ordinary. It's quite expensive lingerie."

"Right. Well, ma'am, I'm afraid there isn't much we can do. It was probably some teenage prank. Unless you think you might have a stalker."

I exhaled loudly. "No, I don't have a stalker."

Angrily, I slammed the phone back into its cradle, relishing the jingling noise it made. I was beginning to form the opinion that police people were useless. I guess I would be eating salad and pasta all week so I could save my extra cash to purchase new underwear.

"I take it that didn't go very well?" Chaz had moved the television to the other side of the room and set it up on an old milk crate. Terrific. He could afford the television and DVD player, but he couldn't afford the stand to put them on.

"No. They didn't even care."

His lips twitched and I could tell he was trying not to laugh at me. "Why don't you go to Walmart or Giant Tiger and get what you need? Stop stressing about it. Underwear isn't that expensive."

"Mine is," I muttered.

It was one of my few indulgences. I didn't spend a lot of money on my clothes, hair, or shoes, but I did have a soft spot for pretty under things. I like lace, satin, silk, soft pastels, and bold colours. I chose my underwear more carefully than I chose my street clothes. Usually, they matched my mood instead of my outfits. I didn't go to Walmart, Giant Tiger, or any other department stores; I went to upscale boutiques and specialty stores. Chaz was a man, he simply wouldn't understand.

"By the way, your sister called. She said she needs to talk to you."

"Which one?"

"The bossy one."

I raised an eyebrow; they were all bossy where I was concerned, since I'm the baby of the family.

"You know, the one with the perfect hair, perfect makeup, perfect clothes—"

"Rose. Right. I'll call her back."

This time I took a minute to search for the cordless phone. Usually when Rose called, it became a one-sided lecture on all my shortcomings. I'd much rather put her on speakerphone while I sorted out a few things in my bedroom.

"Oh Tulip, finally!" she exclaimed when she answered her phone. I shook my head in disbelief, knowing she couldn't see me. Her cell phone seemed to have rung forever, I had been about to hang up when she answered.

"Hi Rosie, what's up?" I knew she hated that childhood nickname, but I couldn't help myself from using it. I was in a vile mood after the events of the day and she seemed as good as anyone to take my frustration out on.

"I was wondering if you've spoken to Iris."

That was it? I thought for sure she was calling about the video on YouTube. Probably not to gush about my fifteen minutes of fame, but more likely to tell me how my skirt hadn't quite matched my blouse or some other terrible faux pas.

"No, not since we were all together. Why? Is something wrong?"

I counted the number of days since I had last seen Iris and my imagination started to take flight. What if she had been injured, was in the hospital, or had suffered some kind of tragedy? I hadn't heard from her in nearly a week, anything could have happened. Was I so self-absorbed that I had forgotten to be concerned about my own sister?

"Nothing is wrong—at least, I don't think anything is. I was just curious if you managed to find out anything else about our father. I think she knows something that she's not telling us."

"You're too suspicious, Rose," I chastised her. Trust Rose to call me to see if I had the dirt from our oldest sibling. Iris and I are close, but not that close. If she were guarding a secret about our father, she wouldn't tell me until she was ready for all of us to know.

Money, Masks & Madness

"Come on, Tulip! She tells you far more than she ever tells me. I have this feeling she's hiding something from us. I mean—there's so much we don't know, and Travis probably has access to more information than he'd ever let on. He's our father too, and whatever it is, we have the right to know."

I let her whine for a few minutes while I made my bed and sorted my laundry into a basket. Rose takes a while to wind down when she is upset about something.

"You know Rose, we hardly even knew him when he did live with us." I felt I needed to point out this fact to her. "He tended to his nefarious plants, spent weeks away at his so-called market, and one day disappeared from our lives forever. The more I think about it, the more I believe he was a selfish cad. I don't need people like him in my life. He hasn't been in it for nearly fifteen years, so why should I worry about bringing him into it now?"

I was answered by silence at the other end of the phone. After a while, I began to wonder if she had hung up on me, but when I listened carefully, I could hear her breathing softly.

"Maybe he had amnesia or something?" I could hear the hope in her voice.

"I'm thinking it was probably the "or something"." I couldn't keep the sarcasm from lacing my voice. Maybe I was wrong to feel rejected by him, and maybe I should be giving him a second chance, but tonight I wasn't in the mood to be charitable. I had already run through all the possible scenarios and none of them had a ring of truth to them.

"What happened to you? When did you get to be so cynical? You were always the dreamer in the family." Rose sounded far more upset than she should be over a father who had been lost to us for as long as we could remember.

"Oh Rose." As bossy and aloof as she came across, sometimes I think she is the most sensitive one of us all. "I'll talk to Iris and see if there's something she's keeping from us. I'm supposed to meet her for coffee tomorrow after work anyway."

I heard something that sounded suspiciously like a sniffle and a rustle of tissue. "Thanks."

Chapter Eleven

I couldn't take my eyes off the beautiful little boy who was staring out at me from my computer screen. His dark eyes echoed hope, fear, love, and despair, and his lips were curved into the faintest smile. It seemed as though he wanted to be happy, but was too afraid to show it lest it be snatched away, forever out of his reach. His clothing was clean and decent, but not quite of the quality I had expected to see on a boy who came from so much wealth. In his hand he held a piece of bread. No one else was in the picture with him. I guessed his age to be about five or six, but since my experience with children is so limited, I had no frame of reference. I wanted to reach through the computer screen, fold him into a warm hug, and tell him everything was going to be okay. To lose one parent is a tragedy, I would know, but to lose both at such a young age is something I wouldn't wish on any child. I needed to find help for his mother, and fast.

The letter that came with the picture was another heartfelt plea to take both her child and her money into my protective care. I knew I didn't have the ability to look after a small boy like this, there were times I could barely take care of myself. At twenty-two I wasn't ready for this kind of responsibility. On the flip side, I think I knew someone who was more than ready.

Iris had been trying to get pregnant for nearly two years now. She and Travis had seen fertility specialists, but even they couldn't explain what the problem was. They were both healthy and young, so they were told they needed to relax and things would happen. Unfortunately, nothing was happening. Iris was born to be a mother. She had been like a mother to me while growing up and I knew she would love this child as if he were her own. Of course, I was going to have to figure out a way to get him here safely, and I'd have to work on convincing her and Travis that this was, in fact, a good idea.

In her letter, Mrs. Akiss told me her health was rapidly starting to fail and I needed to make a decision quickly. Since she had placed the boy's funds in trust, she needed me to send three hundred dollars to release the necessary paperwork to start the transfer of custody. I could do it by email money transfer, or I could provide her with the details of my bank account for direct withdrawal. The second option seemed a bit risky. I knew Chaz had a PayPal account, I could ask him to help me set one up if I couldn't figure it out on my own.

Dear Mrs. Akiss,

I am sorry to hear your health is not improving. Of course I will help you as much as I can. Your son is adorable, and I think I might have found the perfect loving couple to adopt him. They will love him as if he is their own child since they are unable to have children. I would prefer to make any money transfers by PayPal, as giving away my banking details seems rather risky.

Sincerely,

Tulip

Money, Masks & Madness

I sent the letter off, hoping it found her while she was still healthy enough to respond.

"Tulip!" I could hear Chaz calling to me through the bedroom door. No doubt he was worried he wouldn't be getting breakfast this morning since I was still in my room.

I closed my laptop, placed it on the dresser I had cleared off the night before, and opened the door to my room as Chaz was about to knock. Instead of hitting the door, he pounded my forehead with his fist. "Tulip!"

"For crying out loud, Chaz! Wake up already." I rubbed my forehead, hoping he didn't leave a nasty little bruise. "What are you trying to do? Give me a concussion?"

"Sorry, Buttercup," he mumbled before enveloping me in a huge bear hug. He held me so tight I thought my ribs were about to crack. "I was worried about you. I had this horrible dream last night."

When he calls me Buttercup, I know he is feeling protective of me. It comes from watching that fantasy movie *The Princess Bride*. He seems to think that if I were to dye my hair blond, grow a few centimetres and gain some weight I would look like Princess Buttercup. In his own fantasy, he would be Wesley—with his fair, Eastern European looks, he actually did make a fairly decent Dread Pirate Roberts. Unfortunately, I think I'm more interested in the revenge-seeking Inigo Montoya. His character could sweep me off my feet any day. As much as I loved that movie, I did take offense to the damsel in distress stereotyping. If I were the lead character, it would be me leading the way through the fire swamp. After all, I had spent a tremendous part of my childhood living in the forest.

"I'm fine." My words came out muffled because he was smothering me with his fuzzy shirt. When I managed to pull away, I realized he was wearing an orange velour t-shirt with matching running shorts. Who wears velour in the summer?

"Well, you know I live by my dreams. My old nanny had a touch of the sight, since she was a descendent of gypsies. I'm just like her, my mom always said so."

"Your old nanny was born right here in Montreal. There's as much gypsy in her as there is in me." I managed to extricate myself from his arms and made my way to our little kitchen. "What was your dream about?"

"I don't know. You were in so much trouble. Somehow you managed to get mixed up with the wrong kind of people. They stole your money, your identity, and even your soul. It was like they were some kind of human devils. I woke up as it was getting too much to bear." He sat at the little table with his hands in his head, looking shaken.

"Oh Chaz, it was only a dream. I'm pretty careful about who I deal with. You know me." I took out some bowls and a box of cereal. It wouldn't be his favourite breakfast, but it was all I had time for this morning.

"I *do* know you; *that's* why I'm so worried. You trust everyone. Think about it. You hang your underwear on the line and expect it to be there when you come back nine hours later." He poured Corn Pops into his bowl and added the milk, making sure the liquid covered the little balls completely.

"It should still be there! We live in a safe neighbourhood. If I can't trust my underwear to be safe outside, then nothing really is." I sat down beside him and contemplated the Corn Pops. They weren't my favourite, but I had run out of the organic granola I usually eat.

"I'm surprised you still think like that, after what happened to you yesterday," he said through a mouthful of cereal.

"Well, I'm not going to let one teenage prank ruin my entire outlook on life."

"That's not what I was referring to."

I thought for a moment and realized he was talking about the YouTube video. Since he hadn't mentioned it yesterday, I had assumed he hadn't seen it. It wasn't something I was about to show anyone if I didn't have to.

"The video on YouTube?"

"And the pictures on Facebook and the links on Twitter! I should have been there to stop it." I could tell by his tone that he was getting angrier by the second.

"You couldn't have done anything to prevent it." I poured milk into my bowl and watched as the little yellow balls bobbed up and down.

"I can't believe no one came forward to help you! I watched video after video. It's like they thought you were there for their personal entertainment—like a street performer." He stood and started pacing the length of our small apartment, working himself into an unnecessary rage.

"It was embarrassing, but in the end, the only real harm done was to Alistair's mask, and even he didn't care about that." I shrugged my shoulders, trying to diffuse Chaz's anger. If he moved any quicker he would be nothing but a blur of fuzzy orange.

"You could have been hurt, or been in some kind of danger, but no one cared. All they cared about was uploading their videos as quickly as possible. Bunch of vultures." He stopped suddenly, sat back down, and shovelled a spoonful of cereal into his mouth.

"You do realize you're one of the people who *likes* to be in the spotlight?"

"That's different. I *want* to be there. I get *paid* to be there. It's all by my choice. You didn't choose to be embarrassed in front of thousands of people, but I bet Alistair is thrilled. It's like he set you up for it."

"Don't be ridiculous." He couldn't have, could he? There was no way Alistair knew I was going to trip and that the case would snap open, allowing the gruesome head to practically catapult into the street.

Chaz shrugged his shoulders. "Anything is possible, Buttercup."

It seemed I was in for a day of warnings. As I skipped along my usual route to work, I saw signs everywhere: Beware of Dog, Watch Your Step, Men at Work, Falling Debris—the list was endless. These were the obvious ones. There were others that were subtler, like when I burnt my lip on my tea and put my cup down in time to see a bug had landed in it. Or when I opened the closet and an umbrella landed on my head, when I went to put it back I happened to glance out the window and it was starting to rain. It was almost as though the world was trying to protect me from myself. The problem was I didn't feel much like listening.

When I arrived at work, Alistair was back to his usual, snarky self—demanding coffee, perfection, and impossible speed. I ignored Paige's snickers when I passed by her workstation in Alistair's wake. The destroyed mask had been one of her pieces, so now she was recreating it; this time, it seemed extra gruesome and she was taking the time to sew the individual hairs onto it instead of using glue. Derek couldn't seem to meet my eyes when I stopped by his station on our morning rounds. This I found strange, since he had always seemed like one of the nicer artists Alistair employed.

"I see your fifteen minutes of fame didn't go to your head, Cupcake," Alistair said to me as I handed him a pen and his notebook.

I didn't bother to answer him because I figured it would come out as a snide remark that would most likely get me fired.

"You're tougher than I expected."

Now that comment threw me off completely.

"Did you set me up?" I demanded, narrowing my eyes and thinking back through the events of the day. It couldn't be possible. I was the one who had stored the mask securely in the case, making sure the clasp was closed tight. I didn't want the thing spilling onto the pavement and getting destroyed any more than I had wanted it to be seen in public.

"I haven't the faintest idea of what you're talking about." Alistair looked like he was focused on what he was scribbling in his notebook, but I could tell by the slight way his mouth turned up at the corner he was trying to hide something from me.

"You're lying."

He put his pen down and looked me straight in the eye. "Prove it."

I took a deep breath, thought for a moment and said, "I will. And when I do, you'll give me a raise, call me Miss Garden and treat me with the respect I deserve."

I'm not sure, but I think he actually snorted. "Excuse me?"

"I think you heard me. I'm tired of you muddling my name. It's Tulip. Not Cupcake or Muffin or any other kind of food. Nor is it any other stupid flower that comes to mind. I hate the way you demand your coffee in the morning, making me make it three or four times before you find it acceptable. Did you ever stop to think maybe you should buy a new machine? You've worn out the old one! In the end it would most likely save you both time and money. And the money you pay me is barely enough to cover my rent and groceries. I need things, Alistair—like clothing, and entertainment and… and… *underwear*."

By the time I was finished my rant, he was staring at me open-mouthed. He wasn't the only one who had been listening. When I realized I had an audience, I decided to jump in boldly and let them all know how I felt about the games they played.

"I'm really tired of being treated like a second class citizen around here. I might not have a university degree or any kind of special training, but I'm smart and I know when people are laughing at me behind my back. So no more name-calling or snickering. No more setting me up for distasteful jokes. I'm not an idiot. Naïve—yes, but not in the least bit stupid."

Deciding I had probably said too much, I turned around and marched out the front door. This was probably the stupidest thing I had ever done, but I needed to be free of Alistair's condescending attitude, Paige's smirking looks, and Derek's pity. Rose was right. I could do better than this. I owed it to myself to do better than this.

Chapter Twelve

Of course, now I was without a job, and if I couldn't pay my rent, I'd be homeless: one of the less fortunate, living on the streets, relying on handouts, sleeping fitfully on park benches. I reached into my purse and felt for my supply of granola bars and individual packs of almonds—I would need to save them if I wanted to survive. I felt a small tug at my heart as I nearly tripped over a pile of tattered rags without handing out a snack. I passed by a man with his dog, using a bit of cardboard as a chair and hesitated briefly before giving the dog a biscuit; I had heard people could eat dog food if they were desperate. I smiled ruefully at the man, wishing I could do more for him. He gave me a toothless grin with a nod, as though he fully understood my dilemma. I moved on before he could see the tears that were threatening to escape.

What had I done? I needed that job. It wasn't just about the money. Iris was going to kill me. She kept telling me I needed a skill or a trade; that I needed to stay in school or I would end up stuck in a dead-end job. I hate that she is always right. But when I was younger, I had hated school even more.

I couldn't seem to fit in. No one bullied me, picked on me, or really teased me. I didn't get singled out because I had been homeschooled for the first few years of my education, nor did anyone seem to notice I had difficulty with crowds, televisions, and computers. They might have thought I was a quirky little thing, but by the time I got to high school, all those differences seemed to have ironed out. In fact, I learned to appreciate the social aspect of being with so many of my peers, watching them grow and change and noting the subtle differences between them. People fascinate me.

My biggest problem was the teaching. I felt stilted—as though I was supposed to have a cookie-cutter brain and learn the same way as everyone else. The teacher would lecture, assign some reading, a few questions to answer, and follow up with a little test. I needed more hands-on experience. This worked for some subjects, like physical education and some science classes, but not for Math, English or French. I missed the way my mom was able to make subjects come to life; she had a special talent for showing how history related to present day events, how math was important outside of being able to count money, and how reading could transport you to new worlds without ever leaving your own bedroom. If it weren't for her, I never would have made it through high school.

I knew she wouldn't be able to support me the same way if I went to college or university. My mom is a smart cookie—smarter than most people give her credit, probably because of her rather unorthodox lifestyle choices, but even I know she has a few limitations. My march out of work slowed to a leisure stroll. As I passed by *Parc des Ameriques* I decided to sit on one of the benches to take a moment to ponder what I had done. I hadn't exactly quit my job, but I was pretty sure Alistair wouldn't welcome me back. Besides, it really wasn't for me: being someone's brainless assistant.

Beyond that, I realized he had *used* me for a publicity stunt, without my permission. Granted, had he asked me, I would have said no. Not to mention, if I had known about it, I'm pretty sure my acting skills would have been sub-par. I couldn't believe what a selfish, egotistical person he was—quite possibly more than his brother, who had probably purposefully gotten me drunk. No, that wasn't a fair observation. Chaz had given me my first drink, Adam might have purchased the second, but I hadn't said no. It had been so hot in that bar and I had momentarily forgotten how quickly and thoroughly alcohol affects me. I guess that's what happens when you're five foot nothing and weigh the same as a twelve year old.

I don't know how long I sat and watched people pass by. St. Laurent is a busy street with enough foot traffic to keep you entertained for hours. As each person passed by, I would let my imagination write their individual stories in my mind. Here was a young man: tall, muscular, handsome, on his way to meet his girlfriend, not knowing she is in love with someone else. No doubt, she'll break his heart, he'll take months to recover, but when he does, he'll find that perfect someone. Here was an old man: shuffling along the sidewalk with his cane, determined to get to the stationary boutique across the street so he can buy his young grandson the perfect birthday card.

Over there was a young woman: contemplating her future, looking for all the world as though she had lost all her options, but she'll figure it out, and when she does, she'll be that one in a million who comes across her dream job and is incredibly successful. I blinked, shook my head to clear it, and took another hard look at that young woman. I smiled as I realized I had really let my mind wander this time. That young woman was actually my reflection in the dark windows of the building on the other side of the park. Of course I would figure it out. This wasn't the first time I had found myself unemployed. Besides the unemployment situation wasn't completely hopeless, I did have a modeling gig lined up.

The street traffic was getting much busier and I realized it was close to noon. There was no point in sitting here all day, I needed to go home and start my search for a new career. With any luck, Chaz would be at a photo shoot or some other artsy thing, and I would have the apartment to myself.

"You did what?" Chaz was yelling at me, pacing back and forth, and waving his hands around like a crazy person. "Of all the stupid, idiotic things—Buttercup, what on earth were you thinking?"

"I really don't need this right now," I said to him. I tried to leave the room, but he blocked me.

"How many times do I have to say things to you? Don't you even listen to me?"

Of course I listen to him, but that doesn't necessarily mean I have to do what he says. Everyone was always offering me all kinds of advice, from what to buy at the grocery store to where to get my hair cut. If I listened to everyone, I'd be fat with purple and blue streaked hair.

"It's bad enough you quit your job, but throwing away money is something else altogether." He shook his head in dismay, grabbed my shoulders and gave me a little shake. "What am I going to do with you?"

Money, Masks & Madness

"You're not going to do anything." I shook free of his grasp and wiggled my way around him. I didn't like being trapped between him and my bedroom door. "You and everyone else in the world are going to start letting me live my own life. You're going to let me make my own decisions and live with the consequences. I'm not a child; I don't need to be protected from the big bad world out there!"

"You gave away three hundred dollars to some scam artist in Nigeria!"

I shook my head in denial, beginning to wish I hadn't spilled all my money troubles to him the moment I walked in the door. "She isn't in Nigeria, she's in Cote d'Ivoire. And it isn't a scam. She is trying to find a better, safer life for her son. I even have a picture of him. Besides, she's going to give the money back. She needs it so she can secure things on her end."

"Oh, Sweetie." I could hear the deepest kind of regret in those two words. As though he were trying to reason with the village idiot but knew he wasn't going to be successful. "You're far too trusting of the world."

I shrugged my shoulders, knowing that no matter what I said, he wouldn't be able to see things my way. Besides, Mrs. Akiss had promised to compensate me with interest, as soon as she could get her son out of the country, away from her relatives and secure his inheritance. I did have some savings, so I could wait a month or two for her to get her finances straightened around. "And you're far too jaded."

"Someone has to look out for you."

"Really? I have four older sisters, I think I'm covered." It was time to change the subject, this one was getting stale. "Tell me about this art show you want to go to?"

Almost immediately Chaz's entire demeanor changed. He was so easy to distract, like a toddler with candy, to be honest. He sat himself on the couch, leaned back, and his entire face lit up in a breathtaking smile.

"It's over on St. Laurent, a small event, about two hundred people or so. They are showcasing new painters from Montreal."

"And?" There had to be more to it than this. Montreal had art shows all over town, every night of the week. Chaz rarely showed an interest unless he was somehow involved.

"One of the artists used me as a model, so my painting will be on display. I told her we would be there to support her."

"Right." Well, that made sense. All anyone had to do to get Chaz's support is to appeal to his vanity. "What time?"

"Oh, we can head over around nine o'clock. The show goes until about eleven. After that, they are planning to do a little club hopping."

"It's Monday. Who goes clubbing on a Monday?" Didn't they all have to work the next day?

"Artists, painters, writers, models." Chaz counted off the list on his fingers. "You know, people who don't have to get up for a traditional job at seven the next morning."

I was surprised at this. Did these people actually make enough money by selling their paintings not to have to work in a "real" job? I had always taken the "starving artist" term literally. Montreal is full of artsy people, but most of them have paying jobs outside of their creative endeavors, unless they manage to be commercial enough, or talented enough to be able to sell their work. It took Alistair years to become established as a mask maker and his primary customers were still party-goers and B-rated movies. I'm pretty sure he got the contract for his latest movie through his brother's connections.

"Okay, okay. But I can't go clubbing afterwards. Not on a Monday night."

Chaz looked at me questioningly. "It's not like you have a job to get up for tomorrow."

"No, but I do have a job to search for and I don't want to feel like a zombie while doing it. The faster I find something, the better. I don't want you tossing me out on the street because I can't pay the rent."

"As if I could ever do that." Chaz picked up the classified section of the newspaper I had been searching through. "You know, Buttercup, there are easier ways to find work. Come out with me tonight and tomorrow I'll help set you up on a few internet sites. It will make your search much faster and the selection is usually bigger."

I shrugged my shoulders in response. Looking for jobs on the internet seemed like a strange way for me to find something. I didn't have a degree or a marketable skill. In fact, I was barely qualified to serve coffee. I was pretty sure the kind of jobs I could do wouldn't be posted on the internet.

"Sure."

"You'd be surprised at what's out there. You need to broaden your horizons and be a bit more trusting."

I narrowed my eyes and searched his face carefully. "Didn't you just tell me I'm too trusting?"

"I meant you're too trusting of people you don't know. Me, you should trust."

Jennifer Bogart

Chapter Thirteen

The venue for the art show wasn't air conditioned, nor was it designed to hold more than twenty or so people comfortably at one time. When we arrived, close to fifty people were milling around, breathing each other's air and sweating in the extreme heat. Chaz nodded and smiled to people as we made our way to the back of the room in search of the bar. There were so many people I couldn't see the art on the walls. To be honest, I wasn't even sure there was art on the walls.

"I hope we're not too late," Chaz said to me as he pulled me along behind him. The bartender smiled at us as Chaz placed his order. A beer for him and some kind of mixed drink for me. I grimaced when he handed it to me, realizing it was filled with orange juice. Unless it's freshly squeezed, I can't stand the stuff.

Before we could make our way back through the crowd to look at the paintings, we were accosted by one of the artists. Shorter than Chaz, with a lot of curly brown hair, he was coated in blue and grey paint. Upon closer inspection, the paint looked fresh, as though he had rushed to finish his work before coming to the show. He leaned over me, sloshing purple liquid from his cup, barely missing my peach coloured dress. His breath smelled of smoke and his teeth were stained the same colour as his drink. If he had cleaned up a bit, he would have been considered attractive in an unconventional kind of way.

"I'm Alix." He shoved his free hand in my face for me to shake. It was so grimy, I hesitated before accepting it. As I had suspected, the paint was fresh enough to transfer from his hand to mine. I hid my grimace behind a sip of my drink, only to find myself scowling again at the orange juice texture on my tongue.

"Nice to meet you Alix," I returned when it looked as though he were expecting conversation. I took a step back from him as he leaned in closer. I was beginning to realize he smelled of something other than cigarette smoke.

He turned to Chaz, who had no qualms about taking Alix's hand and giving it a solid shake. "I'm Chaz, and this is Tulip. Nice to meet you."

"I need friends like you, I'm so alone," Alix said. His voice was shaking nearly as much as his hand and he swayed unsteadily on his feet. Chaz placed a steadying hand on his arm, but it didn't prevent Alix from leaning into my personal space. "You seem like decent people. Almost suburban."

I've been called many things since moving to the city, but never suburban. His comment made me giggle, or maybe it was the orange juice concoction, but suddenly Alix seemed more amusing than he had been moments before.

"No, sweetie, not suburban at all." Chaz answered for both of us. The bartender caught my eye and waved a water bottle at me, nodding in the direction of my new artist friend. I took the drink, even though I was pretty sure Mr. Alix wouldn't be interested in it.

Money, Masks & Madness

"You're from Montreal?"

"From up the street."

"How about a kiss for a new friend?" Alix asked, leaning in close to me. His attention span was a little on the spastic side and he obviously didn't understand personal space boundaries because he was back in mine.

"I don't think so." I raised my hand as he leaned in closer, his stale, smoky breath wafting too close to my face. Even though I was horribly uncomfortable, I laughed. He was probably harmless, but there were limits to my trust.

He frowned at me, turned his attention to Chaz and smiled. "How about you?"

Chaz shook his head. "Sorry, buddy. You're not my type."

It seemed Alix wasn't going to take no for an answer. He leaned in closer to Chaz and planted a wet kiss right on his lips. To give him credit, Chaz managed to keep his expression neutral. At first glance, most people think he is either gay or bisexual. Tonight he was wearing green and orange striped shorts with a yellow V-neck t-shirt. He fit right in with the mishmash of steampunk, grunge and artistic flamboyance in the room. In contrast, I guess I did look a bit on the suburban side in my spaghetti strap peach sundress.

I could tell by Chaz's blank expression he wasn't too thrilled with the situation. Before he could say or do something stupid, I stepped between him and Alix.

"Hey, Alix, why don't you show us some of your work? You are one of the artists displaying work, aren't you?" I certainly hoped he was, given his paint splattered appearance. If he wasn't one of the artists, perhaps he was meant to be one of the paintings.

He smiled down at me and I had to control the impulse to wrinkle my nose. He was in serious need of something stronger than a breath mint. "My work is over here."

He took hold of my hand and directed me to the wall where four very disturbing paintings hung. At first glance I recognized a few mainstream cartoon characters, popular among small children and filled with warm memories for adults. When I looked a bit closer, I realized these iconic figures were intentionally distorted to become things of nightmares: dripping blood, oozing goo and displaying grotesque features best left unsaid. Mixed with these altered characters were images of children, unaware of the monstrous qualities surrounding them. It was all a little bizarre.

Chaz gave a visible shudder. He's such a light, happy-go-lucky kind of guy; I could easily see how this would upset him. I guess working with Alistair for the past few weeks had jaded my perception. In my opinion, the work was sloppy and not terribly appealing. The pictures themselves seemed forced—almost as though the artist was trying to project feelings of anxiety and stress on his audience without letting them come to it themselves.

Alix waited patiently while we studied his work. In the few minutes we had known him, this was the longest period he was able to be still. In fact, when I glanced at him from the corner of my eye, he seemed almost sober.

"They're... uh... interesting." There was little I could say about them, as disturbing as they were, and I struggled to make polite conversation. "Tell me, where do you get your inspiration from for your work?"

Alix brought his focus back to me, his face was serious and his mouth turned down slightly at the corners. He shook his head, indicating he wasn't ready to speak. I sighed, wondering if this was part of an act, or if he was really feeling so much intense emotion. Large tears formed in his blue eyes and began to stream down his dirty cheeks, leaving pink track marks though the grey paint.

I handed him the bottle of water and quietly took the purple juice away from him. Whatever he was drinking couldn't be helping the situation. "I'm thirty-two, when I was five, I found my mom dead in the middle of the living room. All my paintings reflect my broken childhood."

I didn't know what to make of this. Losing a parent at a young age is one thing, but finding her yourself is another.

"That's really tough, man." Chaz put his arm around Alix's shoulders, ignoring the transfer of blue paint to his bright yellow shirt.

Alix shook his head, took a sip of water and smiled wryly. "I'm so alone in the world, no family, no friends. My art is my life."

Feeling incredibly uncomfortable, I looked from Chaz to Alix. Secretly, I wanted to walk out of the art show, make my way home to my cozy apartment, and forget about the entire evening. Somehow, I didn't think that would be an option, not to mention, it wouldn't be fair to Chaz.

"It's auction time, people!" A voice shouted above the din of the crowd. As quickly as Alix had turned on the tears, his entire demeanor changed and he perked up.

"I'm in this!" He picked up a half-finished painting that was really more of a sketch from off the floor where it had been leaning against a wall and carried it to the front. Relief washed over me as I realized he would be preoccupied with the auction and the subject of his sad past would no longer be discussed.

Chaz took hold of my hand and pulled me forward to the front of the crowd. Neither of us had any cash to spare, so I couldn't understand his intense interest in the auction part of the evening. I could feel the excitement rolling off him as he bounced up and down with excitement. I looked around at the crowd, wondering who here would have the cash to spare to purchase any of the pieces of art. The ones up for auction were donations to raise money for a specific cause; the ones on display would hopefully bring much needed income to the painters so they could pay their bills, or maybe even update their faded wardrobes.

Chaz gave my hand a little squeeze and his smile morphed into a wide grin as the first painting was brought forward. It was done in simple brown tones, made to look almost sepia, but with obvious brushstrokes. The first thing I noticed was the tree in the middle of the canvas, large, with bold strokes leading to sweeping branches. When I looked closer, a face appeared in the bark of the tree. It was a familiar face and I could see why Chaz was so excited. The artist had masterfully blended Chaz's features in with the markings of the tree, making his form seem to be a part of the tree, yet separate all at the same time. Of the few pieces I had managed to look at since arriving, this one was the most remarkable.

"It's beautiful," I whispered to Chaz.

I was afraid of drawing too much attention to myself, as the bidding had started and I knew I couldn't use any more of my savings to accidentally purchase this work. If I hadn't already sent three hundred dollars across the ocean,

Money, Masks & Madness

I would have impulsively bid on this piece, even though it was quickly soaring out of my financial reach. Obviously others also thought it was compelling. The painter might not get rich fast with her art but if she managed to sell her other paintings for the same price as this one she could easily pay her rent and utility bills this month.

Next up was Alix's painting. Created using blues and greys, it was pretty obvious he had finished it earlier today. If you could even call it finished. Once Chaz's painting was claimed, he lost interest in the auction process and directed me back to the artwork on the walls. Some of them were really quite beautiful, especially the ones featuring Chaz. The artist had a special talent for blending and manipulating nature to shield and expose a human form. It was amazing.

"Did I show you my paintings?" Alix was at my side again, purple drink in hand. I wondered briefly if he had bothered to drink the water.

"You did." I nodded. "I found them interesting and a little disturbing."

Again, his face crumpled into a frown and the tears began to flow. This guy really needed to sober up, unless this was all some sort of act to get me to feel sorry for him and buy his paintings.

"When I was seven, I found my sister dead in the backyard. I loved her so much. It's not something you ever get over." His grubby hand was resting on my shoulder and I knew when he took it away he would leave a blue-grey smudge behind.

"I thought it was your mother?" I shifted slightly, hoping to dislodge his hand without appearing to be rude.

The tears fell harder and larger. Part of me wanted to believe his pain was real, but a slightly more cynical part of me was pretty sure he was setting me up for something, just as Alistair had set me up for his little YouTube stunt.

"No, no, my father. Dead in the kitchen. He lay face down in his own vomit, on the kitchen table. I found him when I went in to get my breakfast. He overdosed."

This was unbelievable. I looked around for Chaz, who was busy chatting with a pretty, blue-haired girl who had tattoos creeping along her shoulders and up the sides of her neck. From my position across the room, I could see she was openly flirting with him, swinging her long hair over her shoulder and smiling up at him, all long lashes and white teeth. Chaz was taking it all in, laughing, leaning in close, and generally giving as good as he was getting.

Great. We would end up being here all night, and I'd be stuck with the pathological liar/painter dude.

"Right. Your brother. You poor thing. You must use your art to help deal with your pain." I returned my attention to Alix, who was busy twirling a strand of my hair around his finger.

"No, no, no. I use my art as an expression of my pain. I'm so alone in the world. I broke up with my boyfriend a few days ago, my parents are dead and my own sister won't speak to me. Everything is pain. Life is torture."

Actually, I thought, *this* was torture. This moment, right now, with Chaz flirting away, the room growing increasingly hot, and my new dress covered in grey grime. I was bored, sweaty and miserable, and was beginning to wonder if this agony would ever end.

"Right."

Chaz was now leaning over the girl, intimately whispering something in her ear that made her giggle.

Money, Masks & Madness

I bet if I left, he wouldn't even notice. "Will you excuse me?"

Alix was prattling on about some other tragedy in his sad and pathetic life, but I couldn't stand to listen anymore. This wasn't the place for me. I didn't have the patience to listen to sob stories, the flamboyance to mesh with the eccentric crowd, or the common ground of a tragic past. Sure, I had my own issues to deal with, but nothing that left me scarred or scared for life. In comparison, my childhood had been akin to a fairy tale.

The crowd had thinned considerably once the auction was finished, so I easily made my way to the door. The air outside wasn't much better. It was heavy with the threat of thunderstorms and as hot as it had been inside. The cloying smell of marijuana mixed with cigarette smoke, making the air feel even denser.

Once I was past the urban grunge crowd, I was able to breathe a bit easier. It was unlikely any coffee shops would be open at this time on a Monday night, so I decided I would make my way home. I was tired after a long, emotional day and all I wanted was to find my bed, climb in, and forget about my troubles for the next eight hours as dreamland became my new reality.

"Tulip!" I turned the moment I heard my name being called down the street. Chaz was running full speed towards me, his expression grim. Obviously his rigorous gym routine paid off as he wasn't even slightly winded when he caught up to me.

"Where are you going?" He grabbed hold of my hand, as if to keep me from fleeing.

"Home. Where else would I be going?"

The look he gave me told me precisely what he thought of my response. "That's not what I meant. If you wanted to leave, you should have told me. It's not safe to walk home alone."

"That's not what you asked me. Besides, I'm a responsible adult; I think I know my way around pretty well. It's not like I was planning to cut across any parks or dark alleys."

"You didn't enjoy yourself?" He seemed genuinely concerned that I had left without him.

"Chaz, go back to your girlfriend. I'm fine to walk on my own. It's a busy street with lots of cars, people walking, and street lights. I'll be careful."

His brow furrowed in confusion. "What girlfriend? You know I don't have a girlfriend."

I sighed. "I know you're enjoying yourself, as you should be. The paintings of you were gorgeous. Go and have fun with your friends. I'm not in the mood for a party tonight."

"Well, it wouldn't be any fun without you." His sexy mouth turned into a pout that would normally have had me giving in to whatever he wanted. He was my best friend and difficult to resist.

"What about your blue-haired girlfriend?" I hated that a small note of jealousy crept into my voice. Normally Chaz's flirting didn't bother me. In fact, I expected him to flirt and carry on; it's all part of his personality.

"The girl with the tattoos?" He chuckled softly, placed his hands on my shoulders, and brought his mouth close to my ear. "Are you jealous, Buttercup?"

His breath whispered along my neck and I suppressed a shudder but couldn't stop the goose bumps from dancing across my skin.

"No." I pulled away, but a small part of me was telling me I was a liar. There was something about that girl I didn't like.

"She's the artist I modeled for. Her interest in me is for my beautiful body, pure and simple."

"Oh." I didn't know what else to say to that. Everyone was interested in Chaz's beautiful body. Too bad they couldn't see past the shiny shell to the sweet person who resided deep within. Of course, he worked hard to keep up the appearance of being shallow and self-absorbed, but I knew better.

"Her heart belongs to Alix. They've been living together since the beginning of time. I'm not sure what she sees in him. Her work is so much better and he spends what little he makes on drugs and alcohol. I guess she's attracted to the tragic type."

I grimaced. "You knew Alix before we got here and left me alone with him?"

Chaz shook his head. "Not exactly. I knew *of* Alix before we got here and then left you with him. I figured you'd be able to handle his spastic moods."

"Right. So I got to hear gruesome stories of how he found all his relatives dead at a young age, the bodies scattered throughout various rooms in his house while you flirted with his girlfriend. Somehow that doesn't seem fair."

"Actually, you kept him busy so that Abby could sell her paintings to the right clientele. With the money she made, she was able to pay me for my time, pay her rent, and utilities for the next month and have enough left over to start another project."

Trust Chaz to appeal to my sense of charity. He effectively deflated my frustrated mood and made me feel guilty all at the same time.

"I'm sorry, Chaz. It's been a long day and I'm tired. We can go back if you want, or I can take a cab home if you'll feel better about it."

"Ah, Buttercup, the fun stuff is all over now. We'll walk back together. I don't feel much like hanging out with this crowd anyway."

I was torn between feeling immense relief or guilt. Chaz often had a way of putting my desires before his, almost as though he were a throwback gentleman of days gone by. This time, I took his hand and led him down the street towards our home.

Chapter Fourteen

"I can't believe you quit another job," Iris said as she set a plate of oatmeal cookies in front of me. She turned away to get the tea, which had been steeping on the counter. "You don't have a money tree growing in the backyard, so you have to be careful."

"You would have done the same."

I reached forward and picked up a cookie, wondering if this batch would taste as awful as the last ones she had served me. Iris is sweet, sensible, and smart, but baking isn't one of her strengths. It's almost as though there are too many ingredients to choose from; so rather than select a few, she throws them all in and hopes for the best. Sometimes it worked, but with most recipes she'd create a weird mix of flavours that didn't really belong together.

"No, I wouldn't have. I would have made sure I had something else to go to before quitting like that." She poured the tea and sat down across from me.

I contemplated the cookie, it looked safe. After giving it a little sniff, I took a cautious nibble. Not too bad, if you disregarded the interesting texture. It was kind of like eating half-cooked rice. "Well, I didn't plan to walk out like that, but he didn't give me much choice."

"It was just a silly little video; no one even knows who you are, so I don't know what you're so upset about. Most people would be happy for their fifteen minutes of fame."

"If that was my fifteen minutes of fame, someone else can have it." The more I ate of the cookie, the more disturbing it became. Aside from dried cranberries and raisins, there were other unrecognizable bits that looked suspiciously like whole peppercorns.

"Tulip, you need a job. Or, maybe you could go back to school. I'm sure Travis wouldn't mind if you stayed with us while you got your degree."

I was pretty sure she would poison me if I lived with the two of them for any length of time. "I'm not going back to school. I'll find something. In the meantime, I do have some savings."

Iris's expression indicated she didn't believe me, but was trying to be understanding. I wasn't here to discuss my own situation; I was on a mission to find out what she knew about our father. With all the silliness going on in my own life, I had almost forgotten Rose's request that I speak with Iris to get some answers.

"So, what else do you know about our father?" I asked her. I decided a direct approach was probably best.

"Pardon me?" Iris busied herself pouring cream and sugar into her tea so she didn't have to look at me. It always struck me as funny that she took her coffee black but her tea had to be all dressed.

"When you told us Travis had found out he'd been to jail, you didn't tell us anything more. There must be more. Where has he been all these years? What's he been doing? Where is he now? Travis is good at his job, so he must have found out more."

Money, Masks & Madness

Iris picked up a cookie, performed the same ritual I had earlier, broke off a tiny piece, and popped it in her mouth. She made a big show of letting me know her mouth was too full to talk. I hoped she bit into one of those peppercorns and set her mouth on fire.

"Come on, Iris. You can't hide the details from us forever. If you don't tell me what's going on, I'll ask Travis myself." I knew that would get her attention. Travis was like the big brother I never had. He was fiercely protective, but at the same time couldn't seem to deny me anything. Whenever he was around, I felt like a spoiled baby sister.

"He's not too far from here, about an hour's drive." She took another bite of the cookie and swallowed a grimace. I couldn't tell if her facial expression was due to her evasive answer or her own cooking.

"That was perfectly vague. What town?"

"Somewhere south of Ottawa, I think. I don't know for sure. That's the last address Travis found for him. He lived there until about a year ago before disappearing again." She gulped at her tea, no doubt trying to wash down the dry cookie.

I took a sip of my own tea and thought for a moment, sorting through the limited information she had given me. "Did you know where he was before?"

Iris shook her head. "Honestly, I only asked Travis to try to find him when Mom got sick last year. It took a while because he wasn't using the name I had expected."

"I don't understand." How many names could a person have?

"Well, I had told Travis to look for Jack Garden, assuming we all had his last name. But we don't."

"Then whose last name do we have?" I know it sounded like a really stupid question; our mother's maiden name had been Frederickson.

Iris laughed dryly. "Well, apparently, you can give your child any first or last name you want. Our parents thought it would be funny to create a "Garden" family. When they filled in our birth registration forms that the midwife submitted, they had simply put "Garden" as our surname."

"Huh? So our last name isn't Garden?"

"Legally, our last name is Garden, but his name is actually Jean-Pierre Belanger."

"Right. So our last name is really Belanger." I was getting more confused by the second.

"No. Our last name is Garden, as per our birth registrations. We're probably lucky they didn't choose a different surname for each of us. Our mother's is Frederickson and our father's is Belanger. They were never married. It's not that complicated, but you can understand why it was difficult to track him down."

"It seems pretty messed up to me." Without thinking, I reached for another cookie. The minute my teeth sank into it, I remembered it probably wasn't in my best interest to eat it.

"Anyway, Travis found him living near Ottawa, but he disappeared again." She shrugged her shoulders, trying to dismiss the conversation.

"Well, if Travis found him once, maybe he could find him again."

Iris's smile didn't quite reach her sky blue eyes. Ruefully, she shook her head. "Mom told me not to bother. She doesn't want to find him, she never did."

Money, Masks & Madness

My mind skipped over the fact that Iris has spoken to our mother about this and went directly to her unconventional reaction. Our mother had given up her entire life to live with this man outside of mainstream society. She had chosen to live a secluded life with no friends, family, or outside influences. If you saw her now, you would never have known she had lived like a pilgrim for years; washing our clothes by hand, cooking from ingredients she either grew or scavenged. She homeschooled us, made our clothing, and tended to our illnesses.

When we had arrived on our grandparent's front stoop, wearing dull wool and sturdy cotton which had faded to colourless grey, we resembled pioneers from days long past. Within days of entering civilization, our mother had purchased new clothing, had our hair trimmed professionally, and enrolled my oldest sisters in the local public school system. For the duration of elementary school, she insisted on homeschooling Lily and me.

She found a job, saved her pennies, and moved into a small house with every conceivable modern convenience she could afford. She wasn't frivolous, but she saw no reason to continue martyring herself to the past when she desperately wanted to live in the present. Even though she had thoroughly embraced all available technology and gadgets intended to make life easier for mankind, it had seemed to me that she had never lost faith in her husband. She never sought the comfort of another man, or showed any indication that she had moved on from the relationship she had with her absent partner. As far as we were concerned, she still loved him and mourned him, having assumed he had died in some terrible accident all those years ago.

"But all this time, I thought... she seemed so... I don't understand."

Iris reached across the table and lightly patted my hand in a maternal gesture. "She was happy to escape that forest and our medieval lifestyle. She hated it there. You had to know that."

I nodded. I guess on some level I had known she detested that simple lifestyle. "But she loved our father."

"I'm sure she did, at least in the beginning. But as life became complicated, and his absences more frequent, I think she might have begun to resent him. When he didn't come back after his last market trip, it was enough of an excuse for her to head back to town."

"I still can't believe she doesn't want to know where he is and what he's been doing all this time."

I would want to know. In fact, I did want to know. I might have told Rose I wasn't interested, but the fact of the matter was I had blatantly lied to her. In fact, on some level I felt as though I needed to know. Lily might have inherited his skill with plants, but I had inherited both his fiery red hair and his temperament. I remember my mother saying on several occasions I had the same attention span as our father: which was basically nonexistent. Unless something really grabbed me, sucked me in, and held me tight, I tended to flit from one thing to next, unable to make a commitment.

"I guess she gave up on him after a while. She knows he's alive. I even told her about the jail time. Maybe she was just so angry about him not trying to find us that she figured he was better off dead."

"Oh, that's harsh." I shuddered, suddenly reminded of Alix and his numerous dead family members draped all over his house. "Anyway, that's all there is to know. If Travis finds out anything more, I'll keep you all informed." She took her hand away and refilled her empty teacup. "I doubt he will, though, so I wouldn't get your hopes up."

Right. Well, at least I could tell Rose that I was pretty sure Iris wasn't purposely keeping anything from the rest of us. I had a sudden urge to phone my mother. She didn't live far from Montreal, but as each of us had moved into the city to attend university or find work, I found we had lost contact. Maybe I would give her a call when I got home to check in with her.

Jennifer Bogart

Chapter Fifteen

Chaz was going to kill me if he found out and Iris would for sure have me committed. The problem was I really felt as though I didn't have a choice in the matter. Mrs. Akiss was desperate, her son was in mortal danger, and the government was simply refusing to release his care without the necessary paperwork. I would have thought this was all some kind of scam if she hadn't been able to provide the appropriate back-up proof along the lines of pdf copies of the documents. The forms she sent to me looked authentic, written on letterhead, and clearly outlining my responsibilities. If she didn't submit this information herself, she would never get her precious child out of the country and away from her husband's terrible family. There wasn't much to it: my name, address, and social insurance number. They needed to make sure I was a real person in a real country and not someone out to take advantage of this woman's failing health.

I printed the forms and hesitated briefly before sitting down to fill them out. For the most part, they were standard government forms. When it came to giving my social insurance number, I hesitated. With that number anyone could access my credit and financial information. I understood the reasoning behind needing it, but at the same time I wasn't sure it was a good idea.

So, I decided to research the small African country Mrs. Akiss said she was from. What I found out escalated my concern for her and her child. The country was unsettled, and not a safe place for anyone, let alone a young boy and his sick mother. After reading the Wikipedia entry, I pulled out the form and finished filling in the blanks.

The problem I had now was the lack of a scanner. I could take a digital photo of it and attach the jpeg, or I could wait until I was at Iris's again and borrow hers. Unfortunately, if I did that she would be full of questions I really didn't want to answer. If I had kept my job with Alistair, I could have used the scanner there.

The shrill jangle of my antique phone jarred me from my contemplations. I took a deep breath, set the papers aside, and picked up the receiver. I couldn't imagine who would be calling at nine o'clock in the morning. Everyone I knew was either at work or sleeping.

"Hello?"

"Daisy, is that you?" Alistair sounded harried on the other end of the line.

"There's no one here by that name. You must have the wrong number." I hung up the phone, anger washing over me. Obviously my little rant a few days ago hadn't done anything to change the way he thought about me.

The phone rang again, and without thinking, I answered it.

"Tulip, please, I need you to come back to work."

I paused before answering him, taking the time I needed to think this through. This was the first time someone had called and asked me to come back to work. I wasn't sure if he was joking, and I didn't want to make a fool of myself, but the truth of the matter was I needed the income, especially if I was going to be able to help Mrs. Akiss.

"I don't know, Alistair. I didn't leave on good terms."

I could hear him tapping a pen impatiently on his desk. "I'm sorry about that. I should have told you about the YouTube video. Let me compensate you for it. It's brought us so much exposure; it's worth it to give you a little bonus."

I shook my head, even though I knew he couldn't see it. He didn't get it. His admission to setting me up was only a small part of the problem. "It's more than that, Alistair. You don't have any respect for me. You call me all sorts of names, have me do inane jobs better suited to a monkey and sometimes, I'm pretty sure, you make fun of me when I'm not paying attention."

"What if I give you a raise?"

"A raise would be lovely." I did need this job, and if I went back with a raise and on my terms I could hold myself proud. "And a new coffee machine—one that was built this century."

"Right. Yes, I could do that." He seemed a little too eager to please me.

"And you'll call me Tulip, or Miss Garden."

"Of course."

"And another thing—I don't do errands. I don't mind making your coffee, but I'm not going to pick up your dry cleaning, or be your personal courier service. There are services for that. I think my time is far more valuable."

"Sure, no errands that aren't work related." He took an audible breath and asked, "So, we're good?"

"We're good," I agreed with a small smile. I had my job back. All would be right with the world as soon as I could figure out how to help Mrs. Akiss. Well, that and figure out where and why my father had been hiding for all these years. My conversation with Iris was weighing heavily with me and I couldn't seem to shake off the suspicion that there was still something she wasn't telling me.

"And you'll be here tomorrow morning at eight thirty?"

"Yes, Alistair. I'll be there." I didn't remember him being quite this needy before. In the end, it really didn't matter. "But I'm not making your coffee until you replace that machine, and I mean it."

"Okay, okay, I'll order a new one this afternoon."

He hung up the phone and I was left staring at the receiver in amazement. Too bad all things in life couldn't work themselves out like that.

Chaz wandered out of his room a few moments later, shirtless, and wearing worn out pajama bottoms. If he were more my type, I wouldn't be able to drag my eyes away from his lean muscles, not to mention the faded fabric was nearly see-through. Oh, who was I kidding? He wasn't my type and I still couldn't drag my eyes from his physique.

"Good morning, sleepy head."

He turned and gave me a lopsided grin. I could tell he was half awake, and loved how young and charming he looked, standing there staring at me. I was still in my sleep shirt with a pair of old boxers. Not the sexiest outfit, but then again, I wasn't looking to impress anyone in my own apartment.

"Morning."

"The coffee is fresh. I thought that since we're both home this morning we could go out for breakfast."

He ran a hand through his sleep-mussed hair and continued to stand there staring at me.

"Are you okay," I asked after a few minutes. His gaze traveled the length of my bare legs to the hem of my shorts. He was making me uncomfortable.

Chaz gave his head a shake and mumbled something to himself about white legs and sloppy necklines. I looked down at myself. Sure, I could use a bit of sun, but the problem with being a redhead is that I have the white skin to go with it. I don't tan all golden brown; instead I turn into one gigantic freckle. As for my "sloppy neckline", I adjusted that with a little tug. The shirt was a little big for me, stretched and nearly as threadbare as his pajama bottoms. In fact when I looked at it closer, I realized it was the matching top to his pajama bottoms and bit back a small smile.

"So, do you want to go for breakfast? It might be a while before we can go out again."

He turned to look at me as he poured steaming coffee into a mug. "Why, did your schedule suddenly fill up between last night and this morning?"

I smiled and nodded. "I got my job back."

"Nice." He added cream and sugar to his coffee and returned his attention to me. "Are you sure you want it back?"

I thought for a moment before answering him. "I'm going back under my terms. Alistair is an ass, but it's not a bad job. The hours are good, the work isn't boring, and I'm not chained to a desk. Maybe I'll bargain for a chance to learn how to create something of my own. Only not zombies. Even after all these weeks, they still freak me out."

Jennifer Bogart

Knowing I needed to get the research on my father done today, I decided to get an early start on it. After Chaz and I had breakfast, I made my way over to the library to see what I could dig up in the archives. To be honest, the library intimidates me a little. It's like all the books and papers and shelves hold so many secrets that are accessible to a special few. I know that with the advent of computers, research is easier, but I'm still nervous about searching for things on my own. What I was going to look through were old newspapers, if I could find them.

I made my way to the circulation desk and asked if I could look at back issues of the Montreal Gazette. There may or may not have been any articles printed about my father, but I decided that was as good a place as any to start. When the desk clerk discovered the dates I was researching, she told me I would have to review pages and pages of microfiche, but this didn't deter me at all.

As I sat in front of the old machine, sorting through slide after slide of old newspapers, I began to wonder if maybe I was going about this all wrong. That is, until I came across the unfamiliar name of my father. Jean Pierre Belanger, well-known drug trader…

Really? He had been well-known? Now that was a surprise. I skimmed through the article, but didn't find anything I didn't already know. He had served approximately nine months in jail and was released to complete his sentence under house arrest. Unfortunately, the police didn't have enough evidence to prove more than simple trafficking, even though they suspected he was part of a large grow operation located a few kilometres outside of Montreal.

As interesting as the entire article was, it didn't tell me where he had spent the last fifteen years. If he had been sentenced to house arrest, why hadn't he returned to us, in the forest? Now that didn't make any sense at all. Whose house had he been staying in for the two years of that sentence? Of course the paper didn't list an address, but I bet if I asked Travis, he would be able to tell me. Maybe he had lived with his parents even though he had told us they had passed away when he was a teenager.

Of course, I was completely aware he was capable of spinning all kinds of tales, now that I knew that his "special" plants were illegal substances. And if not his parents, he could have easily stayed with a sibling, a cousin or even a friend. It's not like we were always completely alone in our little fairy tale cabin. We did have a few friends who would occasionally stop by. I remember my mom always being a bit nervous when they came, but my sisters and I were always excited to meet new people and listen to their stories. Unfortunately, our mother would often find some task that needed completing while there was still sunlight, so we would be sent out while she and my father indulged in coffee and chit chat.

Reflecting back, I realized that those visitors always came to see my father. They weren't friends of my mother and she had seemed uncomfortable whenever they showed up on our doorstep. She must have had some idea of what was going on. Perhaps this was why she didn't want to know what had happened to him all those years ago. Perhaps she felt guilty for not looking for him herself and supporting him when things went wrong.

I wasn't going to find answers to those questions in an old newspaper, so I guessed it was time I gave my mom that phone call.

Chapter Sixteen

My mom used to be the least selfish person I knew. Or, at least I used to think she was the least selfish person I knew. She gave up her entire life at the age of eighteen to be with the love of her life. Choosing to raise her children away from the negative influences of society which allowed us to grow and explore nature while developing our imaginations without influence. Everything she ever did in life was for us, including leaving her idealistic cabin in the woods, to re-enter society. She only ever wanted to give us the best she could without our father.

I might have been living in a sugar coated world of fairy-tale memories. Thinking back, I can see how much my mom grew to resent being alone in the forest with only us girls for company. Each time my father left, she would present him with a carefully constructed list of necessities he was to bring home. Most of the time he brought the essentials; occasionally, he brought her the luxuries of new books and teaching materials. Our knowledge of the world came from her, and most of what she knew came from books. She barely had a high school diploma, but she had strived to give us a better education than we would have received in a traditional public school.

The problem was she chose to teach us about things that interested her. History, literature, art, and some biology were at the top of her list of interests. Aside from counting, simple addition, subtraction, and the basics of multiplication and division, we didn't even know that math could be taught as a subject all on its own. As limited as my math skills are, I do know that something wasn't adding up.

Iris did a lot of the teaching for Lily and me the moment she was advanced enough to be able to pass on her knowledge. Daisy ended up being the one who made our meals and tended to our domestic needs. Rose was a bit of a princess, caught in the middle, she wasn't really old enough for a lot of responsibility, but at the same time she wasn't so young that she couldn't be of use. She tended to be our mother's constant companion. By the time I was seven, my mom had managed to divide up the household chores to the point that she barely had to lift a finger. We weren't abused or in any way mistreated. In fact, she taught us the value of hard work, but in the end, it seemed like her sadness at being secluded became all-encompassing, making it impossible for her to continue giving as she had done when we were much younger.

For the most part, Iris had raised me. When we moved in with our grandmother, Iris was the one who got us up in the morning, made sure we were dressed, had breakfast and a packed lunch before sending Rose and Daisy out the door to catch the bus. Then she would spend her day tutoring Lily and me. When Rose and Daisy returned home from school, she helped them with their homework to the best of her ability. I think, at first, she was afraid to go to a real school. She knew there were so many things she was missing. Instead, she chose to finish her high school at home, via internet classes after which she applied first to CEGEP, and then to University, where she received her teaching degree. This didn't surprise any of us, as we knew she was destined to be a teacher. While my sister was busy raising us, my mother found full-time work so she could provide us with every amenity known to man. At least every one that made her life simpler and easier.

Talking to my mom is sometimes like talking to a wall. Most of the time she zones out and doesn't even hear what anyone is saying to her. Maybe it's her age, an illness, or perhaps it stems from substance abuse (I'm quite certain she and my father "tested" their products before shipping them off to the market). No one will ever know. Our phone conversations were usually stilted and physical visits were few and far between. I actually have to brace myself when we do communicate, knowing the conversation will be one-sided.

"Hello?" My mom's voice crackled through the phone line, making her sound a million kilometres away when she was an easy thirty minute drive outside of Montreal.

"Hi Mom, it's Tulip." I forced my voice to be bright and friendly. The last time I had spoken to her was when I told her I would be moving into Chaz's apartment. She didn't understand the fact that we were just roommates and I didn't have the patience to try to explain it to her.

"Are you still living with that boy?"

Immediately I was transported back into the midst of our previous conversation: the one where I hung up on her because I couldn't stand listening to her dire warnings. "Chaz isn't a boy, and yes, we're still in the same apartment."

"You're right; he's more like a hermaphrodite. Can't really tell what he is with the way he dresses."

Sometimes I wish I could rewind time, find the exact moment she became so bitter and pessimistic, and erase it from her memory. "Mom, he's a model and considers himself an artist. He's not gay and he certainly isn't a hermaphrodite. Sometimes I wonder where you get your ideas from."

"How do you know he's not a hermaphrodite?"

"He doesn't have breasts, Mom." That was the best I could come up with. I actually had no idea how I would know.

"Why are you calling, Tulip? I'm very busy, you know." And here we go. If she can't cajole me into admitting I've made a mistake, she'll change the subject instead.

"We haven't talked in a while, so I thought I would touch base. See how you are."

The silence that answered me spoke volumes. She knew I would only call if I needed something from her, unless it was her birthday or another special occasion.

"Fine. I wanted to ask you some questions."

Again, I was answered by silence. This wasn't going to be an easy conversation. I knew she was listening, I could hear her breathing on the other end of the line.

"I need to know a few things about Dad." I thought this would get her attention but the silence continued. If it weren't for the television playing faintly in the background, I would have thought she hung up on me. "Iris told me he had been in jail, and I was… well… I was—"

I was beginning to feel like I was speaking to a wall. "Are you still there?"

"Of course I'm still here." She sounded like she had a mouthful of something, but I couldn't be sure.

Money, Masks & Madness

I decided to try a different approach. "Tell me about Dad. I know you know what happened to him."

"No."

Well, that was pretty succinct. "I don't believe you don't know anything after all this time. And if you don't know, why don't you want to know?"

Sometimes, quiet is more palpable than someone ranting and screaming. Hers had an echo of resentment ringing through its core. The faint sounds of a game show jingled in the background letting me know she was still listening.

"Come on, Mom. It's not fair to the rest of us. We have a right to know what's going on."

Again, no answer. This was getting old fast.

"Iris told us he was involved in drug trafficking, she had Travis check him out. Why didn't you tell us his real name? None of this makes any sense."

When I was beginning to believe this would continue to be a one-sided conversation, she cleared her throat and spoke softly into the phone. "It was better if you didn't know."

"Maybe when we were little, but we're adults now. If you knew where he was all this time, don't you think you owed it to us to let us know?"

Obviously, I struck a nerve, as her next words were neither quiet, nor kind. "I don't owe you anything! I gave you girls everything within my power. Everything to the point that there wasn't anything left for me. Just an empty shell of the person I was meant to become."

Ouch. "I didn't mean—"

"You never do, Tulip. You and your sisters have no idea of the pain that man put me through. Each one of you is a reminder of all I gave up for love." She snorted derisively. "What a useless emotion, when you think about it."

"I just wanted—"

"Of course you did. You *just wanted* and kept wanting and demanding and expecting. You're exactly like him, you know. Red hair, hazel eyes and all those freckles. You're even skinny like him."

"Resemblance doesn't mean—"

"It's more than looks. You act like him. Your mannerisms, skittishness, naivety. How do you think he ended up where he is? He was too trusting, but by the time he realized the danger he put us in, it was too late."

I wasn't sure, but I thought I heard her sniffle as her voice trailed off. Afraid to say anything more, in case she cut me off again, I waited to hear what else she might have to say. I didn't have to wait long.

"I tried my best to give you and your sisters a life away from the city and all its evil influences. Lily understood the importance of staying away from the noise and pollution. I don't blame Iris, Daisy, and Rose for trying to find fulfilling careers, but you're different. At least they all went to university and tried to achieve something with their lives. You . . .you're too much like him. Too lazy to do things the right way, always looking for a quick fix."

This conversation needed to end soon. There was nothing I could do about how closely I resembled my father, but that's where our similarities ended. I would never abandon my family, nor would I knowingly place them in danger. I might be trusting and in some ways look for the easy way out, but I'm far from being lazy. I wasn't looking for a quick fix to anything. In fact, most of the time it felt like I was taking the long way around to figuring out my life.

Money, Masks & Madness

"Uh, Mom, I have to go. Chaz needs the phone." I said the first thing that came to mind.

This time, her sigh was perfectly audible. "Don't let that man run your life for you, Tulip. It won't be worth the heartache later."

"I love you, Mom. I'll talk to you again soon."

"Good-bye, Tulip." She hung up the phone first, as though she couldn't wait to get back to her game show on television.

Obviously there wasn't going to be any help from her, so I would simply have to do a little searching on my own. I was getting pretty good at googling stuff I was looking for. How hard would it be to find my own father when his name had been plastered all over the papers?

"Are you ready for your big moment?" Chaz asked as he came into the kitchen. I had forgotten it was Friday already. Starting back to work at the end of the week must have thrown me off a bit.

"I'd hardly call filling in for an overweight model a *big moment*." I was at the sink, cutting grapefruit for our fruit salad. All that was missing were the bananas, but since Chaz didn't like them, I always added them separately to my portion.

He shrugged his shoulders and plucked a piece of the juicy fruit from off the cutting board before I could stop him. "Even small shows can attract a lot of attention."

It was my turn to shrug. "I've already had enough attention. I don't think much can top the zombie head incident."

"True. One of the artists I know was so excited when he found out I live with you. He even started a painting in honour of the event. I have to say, despite the poor quality of the YouTube videos, he's captured your likeness quite well." Chaz stole a plump strawberry from the bowl before dancing out of my reach.

I gave the salad a quick stir and set it on our little table. The rest was already spread out: croissants, muffins, and yogurt. It was too hot in the apartment to cook breakfast this morning, so this would have to do.

"Great." That's all I needed: my face hanging in someone's living room, or on display for an art show. Chaz might enjoy all the attention, but I could easily do without it.

"Don't be like that, Tulip. It's a compliment."

"I'm sure Alistair will be thrilled. He might even purchase it himself." I picked through the fruit salad thinking it really needed blueberries, but it was too early in the season for them in Montreal. I could probably have bought imports, but they would have been expensive and not nearly as good. "Actually, on second thought, he wouldn't want it for himself, especially if it could be used as a form of advertising. You might want to tell your painter friend to post his work on Facebook and be sure to tag the Macabre Mercantile in it."

"You can tell him yourself. He'll be there tonight at the show." Two muffins and a croissant disappeared into the abyss of Chaz's stomach, but I noticed he didn't touch the fruit.

"You better eat that fruit salad. I made it the way you like it with everything cut up extra small." I waved my spoon towards the untouched bowl.

Money, Masks & Madness

Chaz wrinkled his nose, but scooped out a healthy portion of the fruit. "You're worse than having a mother around, always telling me what to do."

A small wave of resentment licked at my toes, traveled up my legs, and settled itself in my heart.

"Please don't compare me to anyone's mother." My words were quiet.

Startled, Chaz looked into my eyes, as though looking for a way to decipher what I really meant. "I guess you talked to your mom, eh?"

I shook my head, trying to clear away the negativity. "Yeah. Sorry. I shouldn't take my bad mood out on you."

"I get it. Parents are hard to please at the best of times."

"Hmmm… it's a bit more than that." I let the subject drop, not wanting to discuss it further. "Hey, do you want to drive to Ottawa with me tomorrow? We could stop by Lily's on the way back for dinner and pick up some yummy fruit and veggies."

"You mean do I want to drive you to Ottawa, don't you?" Chaz smiled.

I nodded. Not having a car or even a driver's license made travelling outside of the city difficult. Of course, I didn't need it, since I could easily take the bus or train. Chaz had a little beige Cavalier. It was old, rusty and should be retired, but it had to be more comfortable and affordable than taking the train.

"There's something I want to check out."

"Well, it's your lucky day. I happen to be free tomorrow."

"Great! We'll leave early so we have plenty of time. Maybe we can even fit in a tour of the National Art Gallery; I know you've been wanting to check it out."

As I stood to clear away the dishes, Chaz placed a hand on my wrist. "Have a good day at work today, Tulip and don't take any crap from Alistair."

"I will—and I won't." I smiled down at him, leaned over and kissed him lightly on the cheek. Surprisingly, I felt the tiniest tingling sensation. "You don't need to worry about me. I'm pretty sure I can handle him."

"Sure you can."

Chapter Seventeen

Within a few short days Alistair had managed to make a complete mess of his life. Contrary to his promise, he didn't replace the coffee machine. It gurgled and sputtered even though no one was using it, almost as though there had been one too many failed attempts. Upon close inspection, I could see the spout was clogged; it looked suspiciously like someone shoved a toothpick wrapped in paper towel into it, making matters worse. His desk was equally disastrous with coffee stained sketches, unpaid invoices and random sticky notes scattered everywhere, including his chair.

The building had a strange feeling to it, as though a piece of its vitality had gone missing. Against Alistair's rules, Paige was at her work station, plugged into her iPod, probably listening to the latest Indie band to hit Montreal. She was clearly not into her current design. The monster's features were bland, uninteresting, and hardly frightening at all. I nodded to her, but kept walking, wondering where Alistair was hiding.

Derek's work station was deserted; his half-finished mask abandoned on its glass head. I took a quick peek and was disappointed in its lack of creativity. What was going on here? Derek's work was usually consistent. This wasn't like him at all. Deiter's workstation told the same tale of lackluster sculpting. None of this made any sense. I wasn't in the Macabre Mercantile; I was in some mediocre dollar store factory.

I found Alistair in the display room with Derek. They were contemplating the assembled heads. Lined up in order of gruesomeness, the ones at the end of the line looked like fairy princesses in comparison to the first few.

I gave an involuntary shudder. Perhaps they had been told to soften things up a bit and were trying to figure out how to achieve that without compromising the work already done.

"I'm out," Derek said. "We've made seventy-three masks. How many zombies are in this movie, anyway? Can't they double up?"

Alistair shook his head and reached over to adjust the angle of a rotting face. "Each one has to have its own personality. This is the job of a lifetime; it can make or break my career so it has to be done right. No duplicates, no shoddy work, and no cutting corners. Not this time."

Derek started to pace the room, his faux Doc Martins landing heavily with each step. Tight black jeans, black t-shirt, black hair—I was dying to give him a splash of colour somewhere on his drab body. Give me Chaz's crazy sense of fashion any day over Derek's black on black.

"I've got nothing left. Neither does Paige. You saw her beast, it's pathetic at best. Deiter's latest is so bland it looks like a puddle of rice pudding." He had a point. They weren't working to their full potential.

"I guess it's time to bring in the big guns, then."

"No. Alistair. Please, no."

"There's no choice. It's got to be done. We need some better energy in this place." Alistair gave one last disdainful look at the collection of monster masks before him. "I'll get Tulip to call the cinema so it can be arranged."

"What am I arranging?" I asked, deciding now was a good time to become part of the conversation.

"Night of the Living Dead marathon. It's best seen on the big screen. On my desk there's a number of a smaller theatre who will do private viewings." He didn't bother with a "hello", "how have you been?", or "nice to see you". He simply jumped right into work, as though I had never been gone.

"Seriously?" I wasn't sure if I was referring to the lack of greeting or the task at hand.

"It really is the best way to get the creative juices going. There are other zombie movies, but these ones are the best of the best."

I shook my head. "You don't expect me to go, too, do you?"

Both Alistair and Derek started laughing the moment the words were out of my mouth. "Yes, Petal—er—Tulip, I do. It's part of your job as my PA."

"I'll have nightmares for weeks."

I was not wasting my time sitting through hour after hour of the walking dead while trying to analyze their grotesque makeup. I'm not a designer. My dream of trying something creative flew out the window the moment Alistair's idea of research came into play. I thought I could get away with using my own imagination, not borrowing from someone else.

"No you won't. I'll be there to protect you."

I'm not sure what Alistair had been drinking, but it couldn't have been coffee. "I'm pretty sure I won't need protecting. However, I do need a list of alternative movies if the ones you wanted aren't available."

"How can you work for a company that specializes in horror movies if you don't even know the genre?" This came from Derek who had yet to return to his workstation.

There was no point in answering that question. I was not going to spend any time watching horror films, regardless of who I worked for. "Anyway, I need a couple of hours to sort out your desk and you need to order a decent coffee maker."

I turned away before Alistair could argue with me. Seventy-three masks, each one more gruesome than the last. Maybe they needed to simplify things instead of making them more outlandish. Who would take those zombie masks seriously, anyway? The proof was in the YouTube video. Not one person ran screaming from the scene when that head rolled onto the street. Had it been subtle and realistic, people might have thought twice before pulling out their smart phones to upload the latest viral video.

Once I was locked away in Alistair's office, I booted up his computer and set to work searching silly zombie movies as I sorted out the mess on his desk. They were easy enough to find, I hoped the cinema had access to the list I compiled. Titles like "Woke Up Dead" and "Aaah! Zombies!" might not be as easy to get as the more traditional "Dawn of the Dead". For good measure, I added "Shaun of the Dead" to the mix, so that Alistair wouldn't become suspicious of my intentions.

Once his desk was back in order, I made the required phone call and sighed in relief when the manager told me she could accommodate my needs. Some days, I loved my job.

Next up, defunking the coffee machine. Maybe if Alistair had a decent cup of brew his mind would start functioning again. Even though it had been on my list of demands, I had a feeling he wouldn't order a new machine anytime soon. He had the strangest connection to this one, as though it were somehow linked to his creativity.

"I thought you told him to replace that thing," Paige muttered as she opened the fridge door.

When I glanced at the clock, I was surprised it was already noon. I guess the paperwork took me longer than I had expected. "I did, but I know he won't. It's easy enough to fix, with a little patience."

I had started to run vinegar through the machine, the way Daisy had taught me to do with our own little coffee maker. The smell was a bit vile, but it seemed to be doing the trick. Absently I wondered if it had ever been cleaned as brown sludge started to spurt from the spout. In that moment, I was glad I wasn't much of a coffee drinker.

"I'm surprised you came back."

"To be honest, so am I." I reached into the fridge and pulled out the salad I had brought for lunch. The lettuce had already started to wilt and I wished for a moment I had brought a wrap instead.

"Why did you?"

I wasn't sure why Paige was suddenly so interested in me and my motives for returning to work. She had never really noticed me before, other than to poke fun at me, or try to make me do errands for her. Quite frankly, it wasn't any of her business and I decided to tell her so.

Fortunately for me, Alistair saved me the trouble of having to answer. "She's part of the team here, at the Macabre Mercantile, Paige. We need her. I need her. She keeps things organized, has valuable input and is pretty much the only assistant I've had that I actually *like*."

I hadn't been expecting any kind of praise, but I have to say, his words sent little shivers up my spine. Alistair liked me. All this time I had thought he barely tolerated me because I could make his damn coffee they way he preferred it.

I turned around to smile at him, but he had already exited the little eating area. I guess his gratitude for my return didn't extend too far. Instead, I turned back to Paige and gave her a little self-satisfied smirk. It felt good to be on the giving end of smugness for a change.

The fashion show was held in a dingy looking building, away from the main hustle and bustle of Montreal's night life, but close enough that we could all go out and party afterwards if we chose. Uncomfortable looking folding chairs were set up along a makeshift runway and a curtain had been hung for the models to walk through. We arrived fairly early, so there would be plenty of time to change.

I wasn't expecting anything spectacular as the designer was new and everyone has to start somewhere. Unfortunately, I had thought there would at least be separate change rooms for men and women. Instead, there was one small room, where we crowded together, awaiting orders from Leena, the designer.

My hair was scraped back and twisted into a tight bun at the base of my neck while a makeup artist hastily applied a lot of black eyeliner along with exaggerated false eyelashes. On my temple she painted a whimsical design and filled it in with sparkles. I felt like a little kid getting her face painted at one of those family fun fairs. This might be fun after all.

"Okay, Tulip, here's your first outfit. If you need help, ask Natalie." Leena handed me something rubbery. It smelled distinctly of latex—I would know that smell anywhere.

When I held it up to me, I realized it was supposed to be a dress. At least, it was shaped kind of like a dress, but I wasn't quite sure how I would get into it or if it would fit. Frantically, I looked around for Chaz, but he was already shimmying into his scrap of latex. Obviously he had no issues with being naked in front of other people. I have to admit I was slightly disappointed to see he had his back to me.

"It's not as complicated as it looks. Here, this will help." Natalie handed me a box of cornstarch and I couldn't imagine how that would make this entire situation any easier. "You use it like baby powder, all over. It will make it easier to slide the latex on."

"Right."

Again, I looked at the teeny tiny dress I was supposed to slip into. I might be skinny, but even an anorexic would have difficulty getting that thing on.

Natalie laughed as she saw my dismay. "It stretches a lot." She pulled at the sides of her own outfit to illustrate how flexible the fabric was.

Tremendously self-conscious, I pulled my sundress off over my head and started to powder up. Again, Natalie laughed. "No, no, silly. You can't wear underwear under it. You have to be naked; otherwise the seams will show through and will ruin the effect."

I blushed. There was no way I was getting naked in this room with all these people. No way. Not happening.

Natalie raised an eyebrow, glanced from me to the dress and back again, letting me know the word "choice" wasn't in her vocabulary. With a sigh, I turned my back on the crowd and faced the wall. As quickly as possible, I finished with the powder, stripped off my bra and underwear, and shimmied into the dress.

It was a tight squeeze, but I managed to get it on without any rips or tears. I can't say it was the most comfortable thing I had ever worn.

"Oh, Tulip," Leena crooned as she came towards me. "It's stunning. Just as I pictured it."

She tugged the neckline down, further exposing my nonexistent cleavage and gave the skirt a little tug. It barely covered my butt and for once I was grateful I wasn't any taller.

The mirror on the wall showed me a woman I hardly recognized. The teal of the latex was stretched to the point of being semi-transparent, which meant my nipples were clear outlines beneath the thin sheath. If I turned or twisted the sheerness of the fabric wouldn't matter as I was pretty sure my body would be exposed anyway. Strangely enough, the dress—if you could call it that—was quite flattering in its simplicity. Perhaps if I had been someone else, I might have felt empowered by it rather than self-conscious.

Chaz chose that moment to make an appearance at my side. Dressed as he was in boxer-like bottoms, with latex ribbons criss-crossing over his chest and back, I was surprised he could even move. I was careful to keep my eyes trained on his face, since the rest of him was exposed. He didn't have any reservations about giving me a once over.

Money, Masks & Madness

"Uh. Maybe we should find you a robe, or something." His suggestion made me bristle a bit. I wanted nothing more than to cover up, but since he had dragged me into this, the least he could do was be supportive.

Natalie gave Chaz a playful swat on his butt. "She's gorgeous. Why would you want her to cover up?"

This made me blush. Gorgeous, I'm not. At best I'm mildly attractive if you like scrawny red heads who are liberally sprinkled with freckles.

He moved to put an arm around me, but Leena grabbed him.

"Don't you dare! The latex will stick to each other and I don't have time for repairs. She'll be fine, Chaz. She's better covered than you are."

I stole a brief look at Chaz in his yellow getup. It really didn't cover him all that well. At least the teal was dark enough to conceal my most important bits. And really, I have bikinis that are equally revealing; it was the nearly translucent fabric that was an issue.

"After your tour, you return and change into the red bra and panties. For the finale, you'll leave on the panties and put on the red corset," Leena instructed. All my mind could process was that I would have to change out of this into something even skimpier. "Your partner is Natalie. You two will have to help each other, so you don't mess up your hair and makeup."

"I can help her," Chaz piped in.

All three of us turned and stared at him silently.

"Natalie and I will be fine, Chaz. We'll manage. I'm sure you have your own partner."

For a moment he looked embarrassed, but he simply shook it off, gave me a lopsided grin and said, "I'm the only guy, so I don't get a partner. What if I get tangled in my straps?"

"I'm not even touching that," I said and turned away with a laugh. Trust Chaz to chase away my nerves with a bit of humour.

Chapter Eighteen

The show itself wasn't so bad once I got over my initial shyness. Having people look at me in appreciation was a welcome change from feeling awkward in my own skin. It didn't matter that it was all an illusion created by sexy clothes, carefully placed lights, and a general expectation of something spectacular. For the thirty seconds I pranced in front of the audience of about one hundred, I felt beautiful and confident, and that's all that mattered. Part of that was probably because I had been allowed to forgo the too big six inch heals intended for my predecessor in favour of going barefoot.

Afterwards, the models were expected to mingle with the crowd, showing off Leena's designs and garnering interest for potential sales. By that point I was hot and the latex was starting to alternate between being sticky and slippery, depending on whether or not I was sweating. Thankfully, Leena took mercy on me and let me change back into my sundress.

I took one last minute to admire myself in the mirror lining the wall of the backroom. I did look good in the red outfit. The latex molded in all the right places, giving me subtle curves where I had previously thought I was all sharp angles. With my hair pulled back and the artfully applied makeup, I felt like I was a different person, a more sophisticated, worldly woman, and my chest puffed up with self-confidence.

"You looked amazing tonight," Chaz said quietly.

I had been studying my own image and didn't notice he was standing right behind me. Gently he wrapped his arms around me from behind and gazed into the reflection of my eyes in the mirror. Until his warmth enveloped me, I hadn't realized that I was beginning to get chilly.

I smiled up at him. "You looked pretty good yourself."

"I've looked better." He shrugged and pulled me closer to him. I closed my eyes and leaned into him, letting him support my weight as exhaustion began to set in. "Tell me you had a little bit of fun tonight, Buttercup."

"I did."

My response came out quietly. He leaned in closer to better hear me and I could feel his breath feathering along my neck, followed by the whisper of butterfly soft kisses.

"Chaz . . ."

Slowly, he circled around me so we were facing each other, our bodies never losing contact. In fact, if anything, I found myself closer to him, leaning into his warmth. His blue eyes held mine as he bent his head towards me. My eyes drifted shut, anticipation coursing through me when I felt his breath caress my lips. The feel of his kiss was electric despite its softness. There was no hesitation, just a slow softness of never wanting to stop. It was the slightest contact, but it was enough to send shivers dancing along my nerve endings. Once, twice, three times he nibbled at my lips, and I returned his kisses without shyness or reservation. It felt so right.

The latex offered no real barrier between us. His heat seeped through, warming me as though we were skin to skin. The kisses deepened, his tongue tangling with mine while he pulled me even tighter against him. This wasn't frantic, feverish kissing, rather a slow burning fire that spread through my veins, heating me from the inside out.

"Ahem."

I jumped, wanting to separate myself immediately from Chaz. There was nothing to be embarrassed about, but I felt my cheeks flaming to match my hair. When I took a peek at Chaz, I could see sparkles on his cheeks where my makeup had transferred to him.

"So this is the way it is, then." Paige's voice was cold, her features rigid. "I guess I'll leave you two to it."

"Paige, wait." Chaz dropped his arms from around me. Immediately I felt cold air rushing over my heated skin. "It's not what you think."

Even though I was in a bit of a passion daze, his words penetrated the fog. If it wasn't what she thought, what the hell was it? I was pretty sure we were thinking the same thing.

"Paige... I . . ." Chaz frowned in thought and took a step towards her.

"Don't bother." As angry as she was, I was surprised she could choke out those words. She turned on her six inch heels and fled from the room.

Chaz turned back to me, his eyes pleading with me for understanding. I shook my head, grabbed my clothes and pulled my sundress over the uncomfortable latex. There was no way I was changing in front of him and I needed to put on something a bit more concealing.

"Buttercup... that wasn't supposed to happen."

A dry choking sound escaped my throat, something between a sob and a harsh laugh. "Great. Just great."

"It's not like Paige and I are seeing each other. I invited her because I thought she would get a kick out of the fashion and maybe try something like this herself. She's not terribly happy making masks for Alistair."

"Obviously Paige thought differently, so you must have done or said something to make her think it would be a date." Under my loose fitting sundress I was trying to wriggle out of the latex corset, not an easy feat, especially when most of the cornstarch had washed away. My embarrassment was ebbing and I was now hovering between anger and annoyance.

Chaz turned his back to me, offering a bit of privacy so I could wriggle my way out of the rubbery fabric more easily. Even with his slumped shoulders, he still looked delicious in his bright green outfit.

"I swear, I didn't ask her to be my date or anything. I asked her if she would be interested in the show and maybe a few drinks at a club afterwards."

"Uh… yeah… see, now that sounds like a date to me."

Chaz turned around to face me without asking if I was finished changing. He may have gotten a flash of leg as I pulled the skirt of my dress down—obviously nothing he hadn't seen before.

"If I wanted to go on a date, I would have invited her for dinner, not to sit and watch me prance up and down a runway."

"I'd hardly call it a runway," I muttered. The magic of the evening had shattered into a million shards of hope and regret all because of a few simple kisses.

"Tulip, I'm sorry. This wasn't meant to happen—"

"You're right, this wasn't meant to happen." Carefully, I hung my outfit on the padded hanger and replaced it on the rack. I grabbed my purse, checked to see if I had my metro pass, and started for the door.

Chaz grabbed my arm and my already alert senses flamed to life again. "Give me a minute to change and I'll take you home."

I shook my head. "I think it's best if I find my own way home. A little space might be a good thing."

He let go with a grimace. It wasn't in his nature to let any woman wander the city alone.

"I'll be fine. It's still early for a Friday."

"What about tomorrow? Do you still want me to drive you to Ottawa?"

"Let's see how things are in the morning."

Of course we would still go to Ottawa. We would get up early, I would make him breakfast and he'd drive me to the address I had secreted away in my purse on a yellow sticky note. I wasn't about to let a few "heat of the moment" kisses affect our friendship; I just needed a little space to clear my head.

With all the excitement of going back to work and the fashion show, I hadn't had time to check my email. When I arrived home, I found I was restless, so I made myself a cup of tea and settled down in front of my computer. Perhaps Mrs. Akiss's problems could distract me from my own.

I didn't have a message from Mrs. Akiss, instead I had a message from PayPal telling me a large sum of money had been transferred to my account but was on hold pending a Western Union money transfer. I had already sent Mrs. Akiss the original three hundred she said she needed to complete the transfer of her funds, so I didn't quite understand what was going on here.

I read the email carefully, to make sure I wasn't missing anything. I didn't have another three hundred dollars to send her in order to release her payment to me. As I was about to send her a reply explaining my situation, my email refreshed and I received another message, this time from a collections lawyer on behalf of Mrs. Akiss.

As I read it, I could feel the blood draining from my face and settling in a pool of nausea in my stomach. Perspiration started to bead on my forehead but it didn't have anything to do with the heat of the apartment. My mind couldn't process what I was reading as fast as my body could; it was the strangest sensation.

Dear T. Garden,

This message was Originated from PayPal. The Buyer is a Verified PayPal member and he has already send the payment of 900 000 900 USD to your PayPal account. So it's important we know the status of the Money Transfer otherwise, Legal Action will be taken against you. Since you have not replied to the confirmation of payment made to your PayPal account by a PayPal member (Mrs. Akiss) over time.

We request for the Money Transfer Control Number (MTCN) to proof the Money Transfer of $900.00 USD in less than 12 hours and we shall fund your money into your Account or Face the consequences of LEGAL ACTION. If you fail to send the Transfer Fee TODAY, we shall be forwarding all your contact details to the FBI for Arrest and also Sue you to Court as we have the right to Protect our verified member from internet Scam.

Money, Masks & Madness

NOTE: Failure to respond to this email means your Name and Address will be forwarded to the law enforcement Agency, which may result to an Arrest, because you are practicing Scam, and your Account with PayPal will be BLOCKED.

Sincerely,

Your PayPal Team

How had the amount gone from three hundred to nine hundred dollars? What legal action could they take? I hadn't asked for the money, nor had I received anything. I had sent funds using my PayPal account to help secure the paperwork necessary for the transfer. I didn't have nine hundred dollars. Three hundred had been a stretch, but this was beyond my reach. I didn't want to go to jail for trying to help someone. What would my mother say to that? It would give her one more reason to hate me as much as she hates my father.

Trying desperately not to panic, I reread the email, looking for loopholes. Something about it didn't ring true. Aside from the horrible grammar and spelling mistakes, I couldn't seem to find any way out of it. Maybe Iris would be able to lend it to me or possibly Daisy. There's no way Rose could. Despite her outward appearance, her job prospects hadn't been much better than mine. Short of prostituting myself, I couldn't come up with any other way to get my hands on that kind of money in such a short amount of time.

The jingle of keys and rattling of the door alerted me to Chaz's return. Hastily, I wiped the tears from my cheeks, pulled up a random internet page, and tried to look completely absorbed in what I was doing. Of course, I was sitting in the dark clutching a cold cup of tea, but Chaz probably wouldn't notice that.

"Why are you still up? Is everything all right?"

He approached slowly, as though I were a timid animal he didn't want to frighten. I could tell the moment it registered with him that I had been crying. With my pale skin, the red blotches were impossible to hide, even in low light. Gingerly he sat down by my feet, which were propped on the couch.

"Are you still upset about tonight?"

I shook my head, with the drama unfolding inside my laptop, tonight's little event seemed like the shadow of a distant memory. It wasn't even noteworthy. How could I tell my best friend I was going to jail?

"Did something happen on your way home?" He shifted his weight, trying to come a bit closer to me. "I knew I should have come with you."

Again, I shook my head in answer. I couldn't seem to find the words.

"Is it Iris? Daisy? Lily? Your mom? Did your mom say something to you?"

"No. It's nothing like that. I just… I . . ."

How could I tell him what a stupid, idiotic fool I'd been? I had thought I could save the world via an internet scam and had somehow gone from being the scammee to becoming the scammer. I was such an idiot.

"Come on, Buttercup. Something has you upset enough to cry. Turn off that machine and tell me what's going on." He reached for the laptop, but I clutched it to me protectively. "Now you're being ridiculous."

I shrugged, clicked back to my email and handed him the laptop. "Here, read it."

Money, Masks & Madness

Chaz scanned the message and started chuckling. This wasn't the reaction I had expected.

"I'm going to jail, Chaz. I don't have that kind of money."

"No. You aren't, Buttercup. Besides, I wouldn't let anyone take you away." He slid closer to me and wrapped an arm around my shoulder. "It's a phishing scam. Ignore it."

"It's not," I whispered. "I already sent her three hundred dollars, now if I don't send the rest they're going to take legal action."

"Listen, I don't know what you've managed to get yourself into, but this is a scam. I bet the original message from PayPal wasn't even from them."

Without asking, he clicked through my messages until he found the one he was talking about. Sure enough a closer look at the email address proved it had been sent by a third party.

"I don't understand."

"It's simple. This "Mrs. Akiss" has sold you some sob story to enlist your help. She managed to get you to send her some money for whatever cause she—actually, probably *he*—needs help with. You sent it via PayPal, which gave her access to a tiny bit of information. But don't worry. PayPal has checks and balances for this kind of thing."

"But Chaz, the money has already been transferred. It says so in the email. I'm so going to jail." I couldn't believe how helpless I felt.

"Oh, Buttercup, you're not going to jail. The FBI is in the States, so they aren't about to track you down anytime soon. All you have to do is call PayPal and ask them; they even gave you a fake transaction number so you'd feel safe, right after telling you *not* to contact PayPal."

"Huh?" I was more confused than ever.

"Think about it. Why would PayPal send you an email asking you to transfer money using Western Union? Now that doesn't make any sense."

His words were starting to sink in, sifting their way through the fog in my brain and finding that place where logic resides. "You're right, that doesn't make any sense. Neither does involving the FBI, we don't have them here."

"That's my girl," he leaned over to give me a quick hug but hesitated, as though he felt he needed permission.

I leaned into him, inhaled his familiar sent, and wrapped my arms around his neck in the warmest, friendliest hug I could manage.

"We're okay?" he asked me, pulling back enough to look into my eyes.

My heart did a little hiccup at the sincerity in his voice. Maybe he had misled Paige and maybe I had been swept away by the moment, but the one thing I did know was that I wouldn't want to let anyone get in the way of my friendship with Chaz. Especially someone like Paige. In the few weeks I had known her, she hadn't done me any favours.

"Yeah. We're okay. I could never stay upset with you. You're the glue that keeps me together."

Chapter Nineteen

I awoke to the unfamiliar smell of something burning. Without thinking, I threw off the sheet and tore out of my bedroom, not caring that the sleep shirt I was wearing was nearly as translucent as the latex had been. Our small apartment was hazy, but the smoke detector had yet to sound its alarm.

"Chaz!" I yelled and turned to pound on his door. We needed to get out of here fast.

"It's okay, Buttercup." He popped his head from around the corner of our little kitchenette. "I thought I'd surprise you with breakfast."

I coughed and waved smoke from my face. "What are you burn—cooking?"

"Oil, mostly." He waved the spatula in the air and gave me a rueful grin. "I was planning on making pancakes, but I guess I let the pan get too hot. It's a good thing the smoke detector didn't go off."

No sooner did the words leave his mouth than the shrill alarm sounded, alerting everyone in the building of our non-fire. We weren't about to make any friends by waking them up suddenly at six in the morning on a Saturday. At least it wasn't minus twenty with two feet of snow on the ground, like the last time.

"Turn off the stove and let's go," I yelled over the shrill pitch of the alarm.

"Go where?"

"Apologize to our neighbours." I grabbed a blanket off the couch, threw it over my shoulders, and headed to the door. It was one thing to prance half naked at a fashion show, quite another to knock on your neighbour's door scantily clad.

"Huh?" Chad continued to stand under the smoke detector, waving the spatula at it in an attempt to quiet it.

"They're going to be pretty annoyed at their early morning wake up call."

"Uh... Tulip... I can't . . ." He looked down at himself and back at me. Wearing only a pair of boxers, he was more indecent than I was.

"Give it up, Chaz. You're not that modest." There was a castoff sweatshirt on the arm of a chair that I picked up and threw at him. "Let's go."

Apologies and breakfast out of the way, we climbed into Chaz's Cavalier and headed out of the city. If the car had had air-conditioning, it might have been an enjoyable ride. Instead, we rolled down the windows and enjoyed the silence that settled between us out of necessity. I don't think either one of us had the energy to spend on yelling at each other over the sound of the wind.

A few kilometres east of Ottawa, I had Chaz pull over so we could consult the map. The winding country roads weren't always clearly marked and neither one of us was familiar with this area.

Money, Masks & Madness

"Where are we going?"

"To see my father." I was surprised it took him this long to ask what needed to be accomplished before going to the museum.

"I thought your father was in jail." Chaz looked genuinely confused.

"He was, but that was a long time ago, like fifteen years ago. Now he lives at this address, and I want to see him."

"What if he doesn't want to see you?"

I'd already entertained that thought, which is why I hadn't called in advance. If he was there I would introduce myself and see how things went. If he wasn't, we would simply carry on with our plans for the day.

"It's not like I'm going to give him a choice."

"Right." Chaz started the car, put it into gear and merged back onto the highway. I had about fifteen minutes to gather up my courage before I faced the man who had broken my mother.

It turned out my dad didn't live in the country; rather it was a small town, complete with a local variety store, dollar store, and hints of other civilization creeping in. Neither McDonald's nor Tim Horton's had invaded the area, but you could tell they would soon be on their way. Two cars sat in the driveway, the sun glinting off their windshields. Beside them were two kids' bikes, lying helter-skelter, abandoned by their owners.

"Are you sure about this?" Chaz asked, as we realized it was obvious someone was home.

I shook my head. "From the looks of things, it's possible I have the wrong address."

From the angle we had parked, we could see a wooden play structure, complete with swings and a slide in the backyard. If it had been old and worn, I wouldn't have thought anything of it, but it was obviously well maintained. Tonka trucks littered the sandbox beside it. All that was missing was the shrill laughter of children at play.

I wanted to pause, like they do in the movies and make the moment dramatic, so I would remember it always, but before I even had a chance to ring the bell, two little boys tumbled out the front door. I think they were as surprised to see me as I was to see them.

"Mom! Mom! Someone's here!" the older of the two yelled, before dashing past me in search of his bike. The younger one, a replica of what had to be his sibling, followed suit. Blond haired, blue eyed, cute little boys; they could have easily passed for Rose's siblings.

The woman who came to the door was also fair, with light brown hair and blue eyes. She smiled warmly, but kept the screen door between us as a barrier.

"Hi, I'm looking for Jean-Pierre Belanger, but I think I might have the wrong address." The words tumbled from my mouth. He couldn't possibly live here, with this woman and these children.

"No, you have the right address," the woman returned. A distinct look of wariness settled over her features, as though she was familiar with strangers asking for that man. "Give me a minute and I'll go get him."

My breath escaped in a rush the moment her back was turned and I thought I was going to pass out as the world began to close in around me. Chaz put a supportive arm around my waist, lending me his strength.

"Easy, Buttercup," he whispered in my ear. "You don't have to do this. We can leave."

I got control of myself, straightened up, and shook my head to clear away the fog. "I want to do this. I need to. Maybe he's not the right Jean-Pierre Belanger—it's a common enough French name."

A man appeared at the door, but he wasn't anything like I had been expecting. His hair was snowy white, peppered with darker streaks, he was tall and slender, and his eyes were the same unmistakable blue as Lily's.

"Can I help you?" I thought, if nothing else, I might remember his voice, but I didn't. The faint French accent, the resonant tone—none of it registered in my memories.

"I'm looking for Jean-Pierre Belanger." I think my voice might have been shaking, but the blood pounding in my ears was so loud I couldn't be sure.

"That's me."

I narrowed my eyes, looking for a hint of the man I had thought to be my father. No red hair, no hazel eyes—this couldn't be him.

"Also known as Jack Garden?"

He nodded. This wasn't possible. What the hell was going on here?

"You lived in a cabin, with Jane and her five children?" Now I think I was beginning to sound ridiculous, but I pressed on. "Were picked up for drug—"

The screen door flew open, forcing Chaz and me to take a step back.

"Who are you?" The words weren't so weary anymore. They were demanding, clearly demonstrating his impatience.

I looked at Chaz, hoping he could lend me some self-confidence and grabbed hold of his hand for a bit of extra support before blurting out, "I'm your daughter, Tulip."

Slowly the man came towards me and studied my features, looking for something to recognize. I probably didn't resemble the scrawny six year old he had last seen. My two front teeth had grown in, my hair was less frizzy, and I was a good two feet taller than I had been.

"How did you find me?"

Now that was a strange question to ask after all these years. I had expected a bear hug, maybe a few tears and perhaps a "how are your mother and sisters".

"My brother-in-law is a detective for the SQ. Iris asked him to find you."

He nodded and looked off into the distance as though he were expecting the others to show up any minute. His silence was killing me. Behind me, I could tell Chaz was getting restless. This wasn't quite what he had envisioned for his trip to Ottawa.

"I wanted to see you. You know, to… uh… to see how you are."

"You're Tulip?" He came closer, continuing to stare at me. I took the opportunity to study him further. My mother must have been having an off day to tell me I look so much like my father. He didn't even have a freckle in sight to lay claim to.

I nodded.

"The rest don't know I'm here." I don't know why I told him that, I guess I wanted him to feel comfortable in knowing he wasn't about to be bombarded by all his little flowers at once.

He shook his head as though to clear it and stepped aside, motioning for us to come in. "Well, come on in. There's no point in us having this reunion on the front step."

I stole a quick glance back at Chaz, who shrugged his shoulders and followed me inside.

The house was old and small, but newly renovated with gleaming white tiles in the kitchen and bamboo floors throughout the main floor. Tastefully decorated to be inviting and warm, I immediately felt at ease as we were led into the family room.

"I'd like you to meet my wife, Anna," my father said as Anna took a seat beside him.

His wife? How could that be? "And the boys we saw earlier?"

"Our sons."

He didn't seem the least bit uncomfortable revealing this to me. In fact, his voice was laced with pride. It was no secret that my parents hadn't been legally married, but I thought with five kids between them, they would have had some kind of lasting relationship. He had replaced us.

"Hello, Anna," I said, hesitation obvious in my voice. Words were now failing me. I wasn't anticipating him having an entirely new family. "Uh... this is Chaz. My... um... a friend."

I took a deep breath, trying to calm my nervous heart.

"Well, Tulip, I'm guessing you have some questions." He seemed so at ease with the entire situation, as though he had been forewarned that I was coming. But he couldn't have been. Travis had given me the address yesterday when I told him I wanted to send a letter. He knew I didn't have easy access to a car, and didn't travel far from home, so there's no way he would have called my father in advance to let him know I was on my way.

"A few," Chaz answered for me. Up until this point, he had remained silent, letting me manage the situation on my own.

"Actually, Chaz, I think this is between Tulip and me, if you don't mind?"

"Actually," I echoed, "if I didn't want Chaz to be here, I wouldn't have asked him to come."

"Well, let's start with the obvious fact that I'm not your father." His words were cold and it took a moment for my brain to thaw out and interpret.

"What?"

The moment I had seen him, I knew there wasn't a family resemblance between us, but that didn't mean he wasn't my father. He had already admitted to being Jean-Pierre Belanger aka Jack Garden, so why couldn't he admit to being the father of the Garden sisters?

"Of course you are. Rose looks like your two boys."

"I didn't say I wasn't Rose's father. Iris, Daisy, Rose, and Lily are all mine. You aren't. It's that simple."

"I don't understand." My heart was speeding up again and my mouth felt unnaturally dry. What on earth was going on here? This meeting wasn't going anything like I had planned. In my imagination, I had seen him hugging me close and telling me he'd had amnesia. Alternatively, I thought he might beg for forgiveness for not being able to find us after his release from jail. Or, perhaps, he might have even teared up a bit before offering a suitable excuse for his absence. None of these scenarios included a wife and two boys.

"I'll make it simple for you. I wasn't with your mother at the time of your conception; therefore you can't possibly be mine." He sat back, a self-satisfied smile playing at the corners of his mouth.

Money, Masks & Madness

"Are you sure? Mom always said I arrived a couple weeks early." I knew I was grasping at straws, but I couldn't help myself. Part of my already insubstantial identity was starting to slip away.

"The Fall you were conceived I was away for several months. Anna here can verify that for you." He wrapped a possessive arm around his wife, the smirk continuing to tug at the tips of his lips.

"But... she said I look like you. She always said—" I stopped talking, realizing she had said I looked like my father—a man she couldn't stand and didn't want to know anything about. A man who had made her life a living hell and taken so much from her.

"I'm sure you do resemble him, whoever he was." He shrugged his shoulders and stood up from the couch. I guess this was our signal to be on our way. "If your sisters want more information, tell them to come see me themselves. I'm not terribly fond of messenger pigeons."

Even though the world was spinning around me, I managed to get to my feet and follow Chaz from the room.

"But... if Anna can verify that you were here, that means—you—you—" I couldn't finish the thought. I wondered if my mother had any clue about her partner's double life. "Those boys..."

Anna had disappeared into the kitchen. No doubt she wanted to be as far away from her husband's past as possible. I wanted to be as far away from this man as possible. All this time I had been torn between hating and loving a man who wasn't even biologically connected to me. So many emotions wasted on someone undeserving of my time and attention.

"Obviously those boys are a good deal younger than your half-sisters. Of course, you didn't get to meet the oldest. He's about your age. He graduated from the University of Waterloo at the top of his class and now works for a high tech computer firm in Ottawa. Very successful for a man his age."

A violent, angry part of me surged up out of the pit of my stomach and I had to consciously squelch my desire to punch this man in the face. He was a horrible person, and I couldn't imagine what my mother had ever seen in him. As devastated as I was by his rejection, another part of me was glad he wasn't related to me by blood.

"Why didn't you tell me where we were going this morning?"

We were in Chaz's car, on our way to see Lily. Once we had left Jean-Pierre Belanger's secret family's house, I had decided a nap was in order. Really, I just wanted to block out the world and avoid talking about the situation with anyone. During our museum expedition, Chaz was too caught up in all the pretty colours to be bothered to ask me anything. Now, however, the car was quiet with the windows rolled up because the late afternoon was cool.

"I figured you'd try to talk me out of it. You're always saying how it doesn't really matter where I came from, what matters most is where I am now."

He turned and looked at me with those pretty blue eyes of his. They were rather serious at the moment when I'm used to seeing them sparkling with a teasing glint. "And?"

Money, Masks & Madness

"Yeah..." I didn't have much to say about it. For most of my life I had thought I was the daughter of a man who had either died or was somehow seriously injured thereby forcing him to abandon his family. For a few short weeks I believed I was the daughter of a felon with substance abuse memory loss. Now I had no idea where I had come from. Oh, I knew the story of my birth, it had been told to me repeatedly when I was younger, but that's not what I meant. For all I knew, I had the blood of a serial killer coursing through my veins.

"Yeah." Chaz turned his attention back to the road. "Are you going to tell your sisters?"

"I don't know." I really didn't know what to tell them. They wouldn't love me any less for who I was, but they would be devastated by what their father was. Having a secret family outside of us was far more hurtful and even embarrassing than discovering your father was a known drug dealer.

Jennifer Bogart

Chapter Twenty

Lily, as always, was happy to see us. Her little hobby farm was thriving so well she had had to hire a few seasonal workers for the summer. While she specialized in organic vegetables, she also had a beautiful selection of flowers. Everything she sold, she had nurtured from a tiny seed into a flourishing, hardy plant. The business had grown over the years to the point where she was self-sufficient. This was her passion.

A week ago I would have said she inherited her "green thumb" from our father, but now I'm not so sure. Lily's disposition is nurturing and constant. Her need to grow beautiful things stems from a desire to create, encourage, and love, not to make a quick dollar. She may have learned a few "tricks of the trade" from her dad but her dedication and talent is what made her business prosper. He didn't deserve to know of her successes; to take pride in them.

"Lily, there's nothing in the world like your vegetables and fruit," Chaz declared as he devoured a bowl of strawberries. They weren't large, but they were sweet and juicy. "If all good for you stuff was this tasty, I'd stop eating take-out and things from a can."

"I never serve you food from a can." Sometimes I wondered if Chaz and I even lived in the same apartment with some of the crazy things he said.

Lily laughed. "You two sound like an old married couple. Next thing you'll be arguing about is how you never have time for sex."

Chaz and I exchanged an uncomfortable look, briefly remembering what had happened the night before. The kiss still sat between us, an unspoken promise of something that shouldn't have happened and probably wasn't meant to be.

"It would be true, with our crazy work schedules. Tulip is usually leaving in the morning at the same time as I'm arriving home." Even though it wasn't true, Chaz's quick answer took the pressure off and we were back on safe ground. Sometimes I wished I could think so quickly on my feet.

"So what did you two do all day? Some shopping in Ottawa? Or did you take in a museum? Of course, I'm glad you stopped by for a visit. It's been a while since you've been here." Lily might seem like the quiet nature-loving type, but she's a chatterbox when she gets going. I blame it on all the time she spends with plants that can't talk back.

"Visited your fa—"

"We went to the National Gallery—"

She raised her eyebrows and looked from one of us to the other. I guess I should have told Chaz I didn't want to talk about this morning's activities with my family. I was still raw from the experience and needed some time and distance before pouring salt into my wounds.

"You two need to get your stories straight or someone is going to think you're trying to hide something."

"We visited an old friend for a bit and went to the museum. Nothing all that exciting. I needed to get out of Montreal for a change of scenery." I guess it was only a partial lie. Jean-Pierre Belanger was technically an old friend, since he didn't qualify as a relation anymore.

"Any reason in particular you needed to get away?" Lily's questioning was starting to get on my nerves. All my life, Iris and Daisy had mothered me, Rose had teased and tormented me, and Lily had been my friend. It wasn't like her to grill me with questions.

"Not really. It's hot, stinky, and full of tourists. That should be reason enough." I shrugged my shoulders and popped a strawberry into my mouth. If this conversation was any indication of how the rest of the evening would go, this was going to be our shortest visit in history.

Lily nodded her head and plopped a thick newspaper on the table. She must have had it hidden on the chair beside her. "Ottawa is also full of tourists and is equally hot."

She started flipping through the sections, glancing from me to Chaz and back at the paper. I wish I had some idea of what she was up to. With a rustle and flourish of paper, she extracted the page she had been searching for and tossed it at me. It landed on top of the bowl of strawberries. As the red juice soaked through the newsprint, I looked at the article in shock.

"Does Iris know about this?"

I shook my head, not taking my eyes from the paper. Chaz leaned over to get a closer look at the photograph. There was no need to read the words or the headlines, my skin tight latex outfit said it all.

"It's a good picture. Quite flattering." I wasn't sure if he was trying to be helpful or make fun of the situation.

"You didn't tell me there would be pictures!" I had the sudden urge to wrap my hands around his neck and wring the life from him. This would be twice within twenty-four hours that I felt the need for violence. I was beginning to scare myself.

"It was a fashion show and the press was there—obviously. You can't tell me you didn't notice the photographers."

"I thought they were friends of Leena's!" I wanted to crumple the paper in a little ball, light it on fire, and sprinkle the ashes on top of the strawberries Chaz was continuing to enjoy. "Iris is going to flip. Rose is going to flip. This is worse than that YouTube video. Crap!"

"Oh, I don't know about that. The videos were pretty priceless."

How the hell had she seen them? Lily spent her days digging in the dirt, not sitting in front of a computer.

Her expression sobered, her blue eyes turned serious and she took the page back from me. After looking at it for a few moments she said, "I'm starting to worry about you."

"Don't worry about me. Life is good."

For the most part, this was the truth. Life was good. Well, except for my near-miss with the law, the fact that I was a bastard, my crappy job working with replications of morbid dead things, and the possible ruin of my relationship with my best friend because a few hormones got carried away.

"You know, if you want to get away for a bit or need a fresh start, you can always stay here."

I'm not sure what had changed since this morning. Last week after the YouTube fiasco, I would have jumped at the chance for anonymity. As upset as I was at having my scantily clad body on display for millions of readers,

Money, Masks & Madness

I couldn't bring myself to say yes to Lily's suggestion. I would feel as though I were imposing. Perhaps knowing we didn't have the same father was having a bigger effect on me than I thought it would.

"It was a simple fashion show. Nothing to be ashamed of." I was hoping Alistair wasn't in the mood to go looking through the paper this morning. The last thing I needed was for him to try to capitalize on my newest public display.

"Suit yourself. I just figured you might want to lie low for a bit, let the dust settle, you know, save your bacon."

"Huh?" I wondered if perhaps Lily learned more from her father than she let on. She wasn't making any sense.

"Been watching too many Westerns?" Chaz asked. Trust him to pick up on movie lingo.

"Actually, I have news!"

Now that was a welcome, if not abrupt, change in subject. It didn't surprise me, though. Lily can't stay somber for too long; it's not part of her nature.

"Well, don't keep us in suspense."

"My farm is going to be part of a movie!"

"Really? That's fantastic!" I was undeniably happy for her.

Lily loves old movies. She gets absorbed into their cliché perfection and becomes so obsessed she has to watch every movie available in a specific genre. I'm thinking Chaz was right on the mark when he guessed she'd been watching westerns.

"It's going to be a zombie western, so while I'm not the biggest fan of horror movies, I do love westerns. I've been spending my evenings rewatching all of my old favourites. Imagine, my little farm being part of a blockbuster movie."

"That's an interesting twist to the usual locked in a remote cabin and surrounded by monsters theme," Chaz said. Obviously, he hadn't watched any recent zombie movies. From the research I had done in my attempt to avoid the most terrifying movies, I had discovered that newer films covered a variety of genres, including westerns.

This all seemed too coincidental. How many zombie movies could be in the works in the Montreal area? "Tell me you're being paid for the use of your property. You know they could accidentally damage something."

"Well, it's a small part of the movie that's being filmed here. I'm supposed to receive a copy of the contract on Monday. I'm sure there's some money involved. It wasn't one of my priorities since this is kind of like a dream come true."

Despite the fact that Lily owned and successfully operated her own business, she had to be worse with money than I was. My recent brush with Nigerian money scams not included.

"Do you know the title?" Chaz asked. I could tell he was thinking along the same lines as I was.

"Oh, I don't really remember. I'm not the biggest fan of those horror movies, not like you are, Tulip. It was something about being dead. *Dead in Bed* or maybe *Lead to the Dead*. All I remember is it was a catchy, rhyming kind of title."

"*Dread the Dead*?" I asked, crossing my fingers in a childish gesture behind my back and hoping it wasn't. I like keeping work and family separate. I didn't need the complication of an overlap in my life right now.

Money, Masks & Madness

"Yeah, that's it! How'd you know?" Her excitement was tangible.

I smiled, finding it hard to believe she didn't know how I knew. "Are you seriously asking me that question?"

She shrugged her shoulders. "Well, it's obvious you don't read the newspapers and probably don't spend much time on the internet, so *how* would you know?"

"I work for the guy who's making the masks and makeup." Where had she been the past few weeks? If she had seen the YouTube segment, then surely she knew where I worked.

"I thought you worked for some Mask Mercantile, you know, like a store that sells Halloween costumes."

Sometimes I found it hard to believe Lily was my sister. "No. I work for the Macabre Mercantile; a company that creates latex masks and costumes, but more importantly, for movies."

"Oh." I could see her excitement dwindling, as though she had been blowing up a balloon; instead of letting it burst, she started to let some of the air out. "So you'd be working here, too?"

"I doubt it. The masks are created in the shop, and then Alistair's team will put on the finishing touches during the final filming stages. I can't see Alistair spending much time on set. He'd be too far out of his comfort zone."

"Unless you were there to make him feel all safe and secure, like the little teddy bear you are," Chaz's voice had a definite sarcastic lilt to it.

"I'm hardly his teddy bear." I shrugged my shoulders. "Besides, this isn't about me. My name won't be in the credits of a movie, but yours will, Lily. Think about the advertising opportunities."

"Yeah, I was thinking about how cool it would be to have all those movie people on my little farm. And actors too! Did you know Adam Green is supposed to be starring in it? And he'd be here, possibly even in my house!"

That excitement was back and I daren't let it slip that I had already met the notorious Adam Green. Lily could find out what an incredible ass the man was all on her own.

"Maybe you should be here," Chaz said to me with a knowing look. "You know, so you can keep an eye on things. You do have some experience with the men from the Green family."

I shot Chaz a look, imploring him to shut up. I was allowed to keep some secrets from my sisters.

"Or, maybe *I* should be here, that way you'll both have someone to look out for you."

"What on earth is he going on about? Is there something you're not telling me?"

If she knew how much we weren't telling her she would no doubt have a fit. All of it withheld because it was in her best interests—and mine.

"No Lily, Chaz is being a smart ass, ignore him." I hated to cut our visit short, but I decided we needed to head back to Montreal to save my sanity. "We need to get going soon. I'd like to have an early night tonight."

"But you didn't even stay for dinner!" Lily protested. I felt bad, but I knew if we stayed much longer Chaz would say something that would force me to tell her everything about everything. I never was any good at keeping secrets from my sisters, especially Lily and Iris.

"We had a late lunch."

Obviously Chaz wasn't so thrilled with my decision to leave, but he held his tongue. We could stop on the way home for dinner. He wouldn't starve between now and then.

"At least let me get a care package together for you. Fruits and veggies delivered to the city end up ripening in the back of a truck, so it's not nearly as good as fresh from the vine. It's really too bad you live so far away."

"I wouldn't dream of leaving without a supply of your fresh fruit and veggies."

As we followed Lily to the backroom of her store, Chaz grabbed hold of my arm. "I wanted to stay. I like Lily."

I raised an eyebrow at that. "You *like* Lily?" Could this day get any more bizarre?

The look he gave me was pure exasperation. "Compared to your other sisters, yeah, I like her. And I like her cooking."

The smallest twinge of jealousy started eating away at my feet, which I stomped in an attempt to keep it from climbing any further. I shouldn't care if Chaz was interested in my sister, or anyone else, for that matter, but somehow his admission that he liked Lily had affected me, regardless of the context. I needed to get my act together.

"Well, you like my cooking. When we get home I'll make you one of your favourites."

"You can't make my favourite." Chaz was pretty much pouting now, which made me laugh. "Only my old granny can do that."

"Oh, Chaz, you're such a goof." He wasn't interested in Lily or her cooking; he was just trying to get under my skin. And it had worked too. I was beginning to wonder if Lily was right to worry about me.

Jennifer Bogart

Chapter Twenty-one

The Macabre Mercantile Massacre Marathon, as Alistair referred to it, wasn't the success I thought it would be. Eight hours of watching low budget zombie films left me feeling more dead than alive. I had thought Alistair would have a fit over my movie choices, since he had been expecting a *Night of the Living Dead* marathon. Even though the ones we ended up with were laced with humour, I wasn't anymore endeared to them than I was the true horror flicks we were supposed to view. In fact, all those movies did was sensationalize death. They removed the gravity and emotion and left the viewer with a sense of disengagement. Death isn't supposed to be funny.

To me, the bottom line message seemed to be that "less is more". The more elaborate the masks and makeup, the more ridiculous the creatures looked, whether they were monsters, zombies or messed up humans.

"Trust Tulip to mess up a simple movie marathon," Paige muttered as we exited the theatre.

The heat of the summer day was almost offensive compared to the cool cinema. Even though the smell of popcorn followed us out the door, it still felt as though we were entering another world. Of course, eight straight hours of horror flicks in a windowless room can also make the real world feel surreal.

"It wasn't so bad." This came from Dieter, who I suspected slept through half of the films.

"She was supposed to get *Night of the Living Dead*."

I didn't have to answer to Paige, so I held my silence. Until Alistair started to complain, I wasn't going to go on the defensive. The point of watching the movies was to help bring creativity back to the group. In my opinion, watching the same gruesome flicks over and over wouldn't lead to better creativity. Instead, it would encourage the creation of more of the same thing. The Indie film industry deserved credit for its originality, even if they were forced to use low-budget effects.

"How many times have you seen it?" Alistair asked Paige. He was standing directly behind me, sunglasses partially shielding his eyes so when I turned towards him, I couldn't read his expression.

Paige shrugged her shoulders and flipped her purple striped hair over her shoulder. Dressed from head to toe in black on black, she had to be melting in the heat of the late afternoon sun. Montreal doesn't have the gentlest summers, especially when there wasn't any breeze to offer relief from the humidity.

"A few," she answered. "But that's beside the point. You gave her an order and she completely ignored you. I know, because I overheard her on the phone."

"So, you're saying Tulip made her own decision to think outside the proverbial box so she could provide us with a different kind of inspiration?" Alistair's voice was laced with mockery. For once, I felt like he might be valuing my input. "Shame on her for having a unique thought."

Paige turned away and started walking up the street with a muttered, "Whatever."

Money, Masks & Madness

"Anyone up for sushi? Zombie movies always leave me feeling hungry."

The rest of us turned to stare at Alistair as though he'd been infected by some rare Zombie brain-disintegrating disease. The last thing any of us wanted was food after sitting through hours of watching undead creatures eating brains, among other body parts.

"Come on, who's in?"

"I've got a date," Derek said. "With a hot latex model."

I turned to stare at him in alarm and caught his wink. Blushing, I turned away. I guess my coworkers did read the weekend newspaper.

Paige, who was halfway down the street called back, "I'm out. I've had my fill of latex and cranky characters. If I'm going to eat, it's gotta be something I can sink my teeth into."

Abruptly, she turned away and kept on marching. I guess she was still upset over what had happened on the weekend. Part of me wanted to run after her to try to explain, not that I actually had any explaining to do. I assumed Chaz had called her on Sunday, but even if he did, she wasn't about to let things go so easily with me.

"Dieter?"

He shook his head and grimaced. "I promised my mom I'd drop by for dinner tonight."

If he hadn't looked so sheepish, I might not have believed him. It's funny, but I hadn't really thought of my coworkers as having parents. Obviously they had to come from someone, but it wasn't something I had considered.

"Right. It looks like it's you and me, Buttercup."

The use of Chaz's nickname for me on Alistair's lips threw me off guard. I didn't have a reason to say no to Alistair, but a little niggle of guilt crept its way down my spine and settled into my stomach. "Tulip. My name is Tulip."

"Sorry, Tulip. Old habits and all that jazz." Alistair took my hand and pulled me along behind him. Not quite sure how to extricate myself, I turned to offer a small farewell wave to Derek and Dieter, but they had already scattered in opposite directions.

"Um… can I have my hand back?"

Alistair turned with a grin, but didn't let go of my hand. If I didn't know any better, I'd think he was afraid I might bolt. Of course, I was uncomfortable enough that I might. I wish I'd been able to think fast enough to come up with a plausible reason to evade him. As we strolled along the sidewalk, my hand firmly encased by his, hundreds of excuses came to mind. Unfortunately, it was a bit too late, so the best I could do was trudge along beside him and hope this would be a short dinner.

"You do eat sushi?" Suddenly, he turned to me, as though he remembered my opinion might be important.

"Yeah, I eat sushi, but not with fish."

"The fish is perfectly safe, you know."

"I'm sure it is, but I don't eat fish." My eating habits weren't any of his business.

"Would you rather go for steak or something?" He looked so earnest. Was this part of the "new" Alistair who had hired me back?

"Sushi is fine, but I don't eat meat—of any kind."

I wasn't embarrassed about my food choices, but it wasn't something I ran around shouting to the world. After being witness to one too many slaughtered chickens, my stomach revolted at the thought of consuming anything with a face. Eggs and dairy I could handle—but something that had actually lived bothered me immensely. I didn't need to see headless chickens or massacred cows chasing me in my dreams.

"Oh, you're Vegan." Alistair nodded in understanding. "I tried that once, but too many beans and not enough red meat didn't agree with me."

For a moment, I thought about correcting him. When I realized it could turn into a long conversation about why I chose to eat vegetarian, I decided it wasn't worth my breath. The faster we got this dinner over with, the better.

Once we were seated at our table, I could tell this wasn't going to simply be a working dinner. Somewhere between the movie theatre and the restaurant he had lost his usual self-confidence.

"You're sure this is, okay? We can always go somewhere else." We were seated comfortably on the patio of a small sushi restaurant. Dinner here would probably cost me a week's salary and I hoped Alistair didn't expect me to pay for my part of the bill.

"It's fine," I murmured as I glanced over the menu. For the most part, the restaurant offered the usual sushi fare. However, the prices had me mentally tallying which necessities I could forego this week if I did have to pay for my dinner. I could always claim I had too much popcorn and have a small salad and a glass of water.

Across from me, Alistair was folding and unfolding his napkin. When he noticed me watching him, he turned his attention to the condensation on his water glass, tracing the droplets as they traveled downwards. I tried to keep my eyes focused on the menu, but his long fingers kept distracting me.

"I'm glad you came back to work."

I smiled. So this is what this was about—a little celebratory dinner. Too bad the rest hadn't stuck around. Of course, Paige wasn't in the mood to welcome me back, so maybe it was best if it was just the two of us.

"I'm glad I came back to work too," I replied. "I like my job, most of the time. I just don't like being pushed around or treated like a second class citizen."

"So you've said." Alistair's fingers were now playing with his chopsticks. They weren't the usual cheap wooden ones you get at take out places; they were fancy black lacquered with little flowers painted on them. "I'll talk to Paige about her attitude. She's a bit prickly, but artistically, she's one of the best. All this time I thought the two of you were friends, what with her being your roommate's girlfriend and all."

Here was that reference to Chaz and Paige being together again. This time the sharpness in my stomach had little to do with guilt and everything to do with jealousy. Chaz was my best friend, if there was something going on between him and Paige, I'm pretty sure he would have said something, regardless of what happened between us Saturday night.

"Chaz isn't Paige's boyfriend." The words were intended for me more than they were for Alistair.

Alistair set down his chopsticks and pondered that for a moment. "But Paige said—"

"What *did* Paige say?" He wasn't going to start a sentence like that and not finish it. His abrupt halt had me wondering what Paige had been saying about both her relationship with Chaz and what she thought of me.

"Nothing. Don't worry about it." He glanced around, as though searching for someone. It was still early for dinner in Montreal, so the patio wasn't yet filled to capacity. The waitress had been by to fill our water glasses, but hadn't been seen since.

"Alistair, whenever you say "don't worry about it", it *makes* me worry. You may as well tell me what Paige said. You know I'll find out anyway." He couldn't know I was bluffing on that last part, but as the silence stretched between us, I began to wonder if he had figured me out.

"It's really not important. Where is that waitress? A man could starve to death with service like this."

"Changing the subject isn't going to get you off the hook so easily." My bravery was starting to waver. If he didn't tell me soon what she had said, I was going to have to give up and ask Chaz. I'm pretty sure if I did that, it would create a bigger barrier between us.

"Persistent today, aren't you? I like that in a woman."

My eyes popped wide open in astonishment. This celebratory dinner wasn't going the way I had expected. "Huh?"

"All this time I thought you were this wishy-washy little thing and then I find out you're not quite the skittish butterfly you present to the daytime world. With your girlish sundresses and wheat germ morals, I had no idea of who you really are."

"I have no idea what you're talking about." This had to be one of the strangest conversations I had ever had.

"Of course you do, Tulip. There's no need for you to be all coy and chaste with me. Your secret's out now." His smirk sent shivers up my spine.

"One appearance in a fashion show doesn't make me a different person."

"Paige told me you'd say something like that. But there's more to it than that, isn't there?"

I racked my brain, searched the shadows and sifted through the cobwebs but couldn't begin to understand what he was talking about. My only other foray into the limelight had been a simple accident, nothing more. The rest of my life was private.

"I'm pretty sure there isn't."

"Come on, Blossom. You're a free spirit. If I'd known sooner, we could have taken advantage of your lifestyle."

"Alistair, I don't mean to be rude, but I'm not liking the way this conversation is going." The kiss Paige witnessed must have disturbed her even more than I had thought if she was spreading nasty lies about me. "Tell me what Paige said."

"She actually didn't say much about you, she pointed me in the right direction when it comes to your... charms."

I couldn't do this any longer. I was having visions of me jumping across the table, landing in his lap, and wrapping my hands around his neck. In my fantasy daydream, I had super strength and took delight in watching him try to wrench free of my grasp, all the while his normally pale face turning various shades of purple and blue. Maybe watching horror movies all afternoon had affected my mental stability.

"I wish I had a clue what you're talking about." Actually, I didn't, but the words popped out of my mouth anyway.

He took a sip of his water, raised his eyebrows and let out an audible sigh. "You know—*your lifestyle*. I'm up for sharing."

I shook my head, still not understanding what he was trying to get at.

"Look, Paige said you kept it quiet because you didn't want people to get the wrong idea about you. I get it. You're a free-loving spirit, but that doesn't necessarily mean you're a slut."

"*What?*" The ability to form comprehensive sentences suddenly disappeared.

"That fashion show and your involvement with that particular group are fine with me. I don't mind that you share your body and passions with others. In fact, I don't understand why you keep it a secret. Isn't it a bit hypocritical to be all about love, tolerance, and sexual spirituality and yet desperately keep it a secret?"

I stood up from the table, resisted the urge to throw my glass of water into his smirking face, and started to walk away. He hadn't changed at all.

"Tulip!"

The best I could do in the moment was to keep walking or I might say or do something I would regret later. Of course, at this point I already had enough regret to fill my belly for a lifetime. I didn't need to add to the pot. If I had enough nerve, I would march straight over to Paige's apartment and ask her all the questions I couldn't ask Alistair.

Fortunately for both of us, I didn't. Instead I made my way home to a blissfully empty apartment, made myself a simple salad for dinner and locked myself in my room for the duration of the night. Whatever madness was going on in the world outside my bedroom, I didn't need or want to know.

Jennifer Bogart

Chapter Twenty-two

"*Tulip!*" I could hear her calling, but I couldn't see her though the mist. The harder I looked, the further away she seemed to be. "*Tulip, I need you!*"

I'm pretty sure it was Lily calling me, but the fog was rolling in so thick; I'd never seen it like this in Montreal. I felt like I had been transported through time and place to another dimension.

"*Tulip!*" Now Rose was searching for me, I could tell because her voice is higher and sweeter than Lily's husky tones. "*Hurry!*"

My head was filled with murky water and I could no longer tell if it was the fog distorting my vision or if something inside me was preventing me from discerning what needed to be seen. Each time I turned toward a voice another one called to me. Iris, Daisy, my mother… I was being pulled in so many directions.

When I thought I couldn't take anymore, a figure emerged from the gloom. Taller than me, dark hair streaked with purple and blue, her features were distorted into a gruesome smile. Her eyes reflected vacant holes of endless misery. I shivered, wanting to run in the opposite direction, but my feet were stuck in the muck and I couldn't move. Paige reached out a hand, beckoning me towards her. Frantically, I twisted away, afraid to answer her call.

"Tulip, this way! Hurry!"

Behind me, another figure appeared. Tall, lithe and unfamiliar, his gait was awkward while his voice grated like metal on metal. As he moved towards me, I could make out his features: hooked nose, blue eyes and grey hair peppered with traces of brown—my father but not my father. I shivered, as he shuffled closer, his face morphing into something waxen and disfigured.

"Help me, please, Tulip," a child's voice called. I could see him clearly in the haze, dark skin, dark hair and eyes shining with hope. His clothes were tattered and his shoulders were slumped with hunger and defeat. He needed me, this boy, but I couldn't remember why. He was all innocence in this horrible world. I reached my hand out to him, still unable to move my feet. The boy smiled, showing a mouth full of rotten teeth through lips tinged green with decay. Shuddering, I withdrew my hand, but it was too late, he was already coming towards me.

My heart was racing even though I couldn't run or break free from the circle of ghastly figures closing in on me. In my peripheral vision, I thought I saw Iris, but when I focused my gaze on her, she was only a shadow of the sister I knew. I swear I saw a spider creep out of her left eye socket and scurry across her cheek. Each time I sought comfort with one of my sisters, her features shifted, slinking into a mask of oozing decay. I began to choke on the terror that was building within me.

Unable to run, all I could was twist away from one aberration to another. They were unrelenting in their persistence, shuffling forward. With each step closer, their deformities became more obvious. Lily was missing half of her right arm and where her ear should have been was a gaping hole seeping with black goo. Rose's limbs were covered in blistering sores; her facial features were distorted, sliding down in a pool of melted wax. I couldn't even look at Daisy, her features didn't line up properly, what remained of her hair was a tangled clump of grime and her skin hung in limp clumps from her skeleton.

"Tulip, what's the matter, honey? We only want you to know we care."

My mother was beside me. Pus-filled pockets of skin leaked yellow slime and when she smiled I could see black tar lining the inside of her mouth. She lifted her blistered hand to caress my face and I did what any sane person would. I covered my ears, closed my eyes and screamed. It seemed the louder I screamed, the closer they came to me.

"Tulip, you're dreaming."

A dark shadow was looming over me, as it reached towards me, I screamed again and swatted it away. Tangled as I was in the sheets, I still couldn't move my feet.

"Buttercup. Sweetheart. Wake up."

The words began to penetrate the fog of my sleep befuddled mind. I sat up with a jerk and nervously looked around the room, searching for remnants of my nightmare. The numbers on the clock glowed an eerie blue, telling me it wasn't quite midnight. Still shaking, I ran a hand through the tangled mass of hair that half-covered my face and tried to regain a modicum of composure.

"Are you okay? That was some dream." Chaz pulled me towards him and held me close. I couldn't seem to get control of myself. "You're shaking like crazy. Want to talk about it?"

"It was a stupid dream." Now that I was wide awake it all seemed ridiculous. I must have superimposed the effects from the movies we had watched today over the faces of my friends and family.

Obviously the stress of the weekend, my dinner with Alistair, and my wild imagination had all caught up with each other at the same time to create a crazy vortex of dark emotion my subconscious needed to work out. I wished it had chosen a softer, sweeter genre. Horror really wasn't my thing.

As Chaz held me close, his warmth melting the fear that had encased me, I began to relax against him. His fingers drifted over my back, lightly caressing me through the thin fabric of my sleep shirt. I could feel his breath teasing the sensitive skin of my neck and I shivered. Whether my attraction stemmed from our growing friendship or the relief of being freed from my nightmare, I didn't really care. I wanted him to hold me close so I could forget about the world around me.

I felt his lips graze my cheek, feather-soft as he brought his lips close to mine. "Are you sure you're all right, now?"

I smiled and leaned towards him. If he wasn't going to bridge the gap, I would do it for him. My tongue darted out to get a quick taste of his lips and I smiled again at his quick intake of breath.

"I'm fine. I was having a bad dream." I didn't want to talk about it anymore. Remembering the deathly images propelled me forward to feel alive. I nipped at his lips again, suddenly feeling bold. I knew he wanted this too.

Chaz's lips captured mine in a kiss that stole away my breath. He tasted of cinnamon, apples and a spiciness that could only be him. As our tongues danced together, I felt all the stress of the past few days drain away to be replaced by a different kind of tension.

I wrapped my arms around the solid strength of his chest. All lean muscle, I'd felt his embrace before, always inviting, but never so sensual. Muscles rippled as I teased my fingertips across his shoulders and down his back. There was no weakness here, only strength.

His fingers were traveling along the length of the back of my neck, playing with my hair, skirting along my collarbones and stopping above the swell of my breasts. I looked into his blue eyes and hoped he read the emphatic "yes" reflected in mine. I knew the moment he did. His expression darkened, his eyes grew hot, and his caresses became more daring.

Gently he cupped each breast, molded, and released it. Warmth spread through me with a shudder of pleasure. I wanted to feel the searing heat of skin on skin. As though he could read my thoughts, Chaz slid his hands down along my waist, found the hem of my shirt and pulled it over my head in one fluid motion. The tiniest of smiles tugged at the corners of his lips.

"You're beautiful." His words fluttered into the air as he leaned forward and touched his lips to mine. Reaching his hands around me, he pulled me close. There was still too much fabric between us. I leaned back, gave his t-shirt a tug, and he dutifully lifted it over his head and tossed it on the floor. Seeing Chaz half-naked wasn't a surprise, but having him here in my bed, with the soft light from the hallway filtering in, made me feel deliciously tingly inside.

A tiny sound escaped me, something between a gasp and a moan as our bodies came together. We were fluid, each an extension of the other. Tasting, tickling, teasing—each caress blended into another, until neither of us really knew where one began and the other ended. For a brief moment, the world tilted, but then it settled back to where it was meant to be. I fell asleep with the comfort of Chaz's arms wrapped around me.

I must have been insane to think Chaz and I could have sex and all would be right with the world when I woke up. That little axis tilt I felt last night was more like a full-fledged topple. Unfortunately, I'm the one who ended up on the bottom. Why is it that every time I think something is going right in my life, I end up being horribly disillusioned? Chaz and I were supposed to be best friends, not boyfriend and girlfriend. Rose would call it "friends with benefits", I'm sure Paige would use the term "Fuck Buddies". There's too much pressure in a romantic relationship. They never turn out quite the way you want, despite what the storybooks say.

He was laying beside me, looking all sweet and innocent in his sleep. Of course, Chaz was sweet and innocent. I'm the one who pulled him into this mess all because of a stupid nightmare. In the moment, I had needed someone to chase the bad dreams away, to make me feel safe and provide me with comfort. Chaz had been accommodating, to say the least. I didn't blame him; I hoped he would understand that I didn't want to complicate things between us. He's my best friend and I doubted I could navigate the world without him at my side.

Chaz stretched, groaned, and rolled onto his back. As he moved, the sheet slid down his body and came to rest precariously below his hips. I was sure if he shifted a tiny bit—

I shook my head and tried to get my thoughts in order. Here I was, sitting naked on my bed with a naked man beside me. It would be so easy to snuggle back down under the sheet and pick up where we had left off. A little shiver danced along my spine and I decided I had better get up before I let the little devil on my shoulder have her way. Talking to Chaz about all this was going to be hard enough; I didn't need to complicate things even more.

Carefully I stood, trying not to jostle the bed too much. Chaz might be a deep sleeper, but he was beginning to stir. Even he couldn't sleep the entire day away.

"Come back to bed, Buttercup." His hand reached over to where I had been seated seconds before. Had he been awake the entire time I was contemplating my dilemma? He patted the bed and I bit back a laugh. Trust Chaz to be too lazy to actually sit up and talk to me.

"It's too early to be up." A quick glance at the clock confirmed Chaz's statement, which made me more leery of how long he had been awake. Even though the sun was starting to stream through the window, it was only a little after five in the morning. Obviously, today was going to be a bright and sunny day.

"Chaz . . ." His name came out on a sigh. Standing in the middle of my room in nothing by my skin, I felt awkward and sexy all at the same time.

Blissfully, he kept his face turned towards the wall. "I know what you're thinking, Buttercup." His voice held no traces of sleep.

"What—?" Even I wasn't sure how to articulate my question.

"You're worried that sex is going to complicate our relationship. It won't."

"How do you know?" He couldn't know.

"Because I won't let it. You're my best friend. The fact that I find you wildly attractive is a good thing. This was meant to happen." He turned to face me.

Unprepared, I stood there, letting his eyes peruse me. When I realized what he was doing I blushed and tried to turn away. Abruptly, Chaz extricated himself from the tangled sheet and the next thing I knew he was standing in front of me.

He took hold of my hand and led me back towards the bed where he sat and pulled me in front of him to stand between his knees. He was so tall, that even sitting I hardly had to look down at him. "I'm not about to let what happened last night destroy our friendship."

I couldn't answer him. Feeling the crisp whorls of hair on his thighs brushing the outside of mine was doing strange things to my stomach. My mouth was dry and my breath was growing more and more shallow by the second. Lightly, I laid my hands on his shoulders, but for some reason, I couldn't keep my fingers still. They insisted on stroking his skin in small little circles, reveling in the softness of it.

Chaz's hands came to rest on my waist and he drew me closer until his nose was buried in my chest. He inhaled deeply and then exhaled loud enough for me to know he was trying to figure out exactly what he should say.

Money, Masks & Madness

"Did you really think sneaking out of your own bedroom would be better than facing what happened? Something like this doesn't disappear because you want it to." His voice had a slight edge to it, and I knew he was upset that I had tried to leave without speaking to him.

"I... I didn't want to complicate things." My fingers stilled, but his started to roam, tracing patterns along my ribcage and across my back.

I could feel his smile against my breasts just before his tongue darted out to have a little taste. I inhaled sharply, taken aback by his playfulness while he was scolding me. "Trust me, there's nothing complicated about this."

Chaz leaned back on the bed, pulling me with him until I lost my balance and landed sprawled on top of him. He grunted softly as my elbow connected with his ribs.

"Sorry," I muttered, but a giggle escaped.

"You think maiming me is funny?" Chaz asked. His fingers started to explore my body, searching for all those ticklish spots he had found last night. I laughed and wriggled until somehow he ended up on top of me. His expression turned serious. "I don't regret anything about last night. If you do, say so now."

I shook my head. Another quick glance at the clock confirmed that we had time. Licking my lips, I extricated my arms and wrapped them around Chaz's neck, pulling him close until our lips met. I let my body share with him the words my mouth couldn't shape.

Jennifer Bogart

Chapter Twenty-three

When I walked into Alistair's office four sets of curious eyes were staring at me as though I didn't belong there. I may have argued with Alistair at dinner, but I hadn't quit and he hadn't fired me, so I simply assumed I was still employed.

"What?" Maybe I sounded rude, but a part of me didn't care. Whatever Alistair had told them must have been some doozy of a lie because the silence continued.

Deciding it was best to ignore them; I skirted around them and made my way to the coffee machine. To my surprise, it wasn't there. Confused, I looked around, wondering if Alistair might have moved the monstrosity. I found it on the floor in the corner. A few fresh dents on the side clearly indicated someone had gone a few rounds with it and the machine hadn't come out the victor. I guess Alistair wasn't getting his coffee this morning.

"The new one is on its way," Alistair's clipped accent finally broke the silence. "Nice of you to join us, Ms. Garden. You're late."

"No, I'm not. That clock is fast. You know that because you had me set it eight minutes fast so you would always meet your deadlines."

"Regardless, since I wasn't sure you were coming in today, I called the temp agency."

I didn't want to play this game with him. "Are you firing me?"

"No. I thought that as flighty as you can be, you might expect the day off after last night."

What was that supposed to mean? From the corner of my eye, I saw Paige give a little smirk. Obviously she wasn't up to any good.

"I'm fine, Alistair. It was a little misunderstanding we can easily set behind us."

"If you say so." He shrugged his shoulders and stood up from his desk. "All right, the rest of you need to get back to work. We have a deadline looming and a few more masks to complete."

I sighed in relief, glad we were getting on with the work day as usual. The last thing I needed was more strangeness in my life.

"Fetch my daybook from my desk, will you, Petal?" We were halfway across the workroom which could easily be viewed from Alistair's office. Assuming he wanted to consult it to ensure he was on track with the designs, I turned around to get it, letting his use of a nickname slide.

On his desk, spread out for everyone to see was the local entertainment section of an artsy rag. A picture of Alistair and me was displayed in full colour. Under it, the caption read: *Alistair Green and his latest fling, Tulip Garden, enjoy a night on the town.* In the picture, his hand looked like it was holding mine, but I knew differently. He had been trying to make a point when the photographer had snapped that picture. I didn't bother to read the rest of the article. The world could think what they wanted, but I knew the truth.

Money, Masks & Madness

By the end of the day, I was exhausted. All I wanted to do was soak in a relaxing bubble bath, flip through a magazine, and go to bed early. So much had happened in such a short amount of time that my brain was working in overdrive while my body lagged behind.

Coming home to an empty apartment was both a relief and a disappointment. Relief to have a few blissful moments to myself and disappointment at not having Chaz greet me at the door with flowers. Of course, I didn't actually expect flowers, but his smile would have been a welcome sight. All day long I had been met with nothing but frosty stares and furtive glances. I was beginning to wonder if there was something else I had missed.

Absently, I turned on my laptop. While I waited for it to boot up, I plugged in the kettle to make a cup of tea. In contrast to the bright sunshine of the morning, the evening had cooled as storm clouds rolled in. I welcomed the drop in temperature, it meant I could soak in the tub, curl up with a good book under a blanket, and enjoy my tea in comfort. Everything I needed to chase my blues away.

Mrs. Akiss was still sending me messages, imploring me to send more money. In good faith she had started the transfer process and now she was more destitute than she had been before. Grateful I hadn't sent the rest of the funds, or given her my personal details, I decided to ignore her emails. Chaz was right; it wasn't likely she was going to show up on my doorstep since it was obviously a scam. I had called PayPal and they had confirmed his hunch, telling me to ignore all further messages from the interloper. The problem was I couldn't seem to dismiss the shining eyes and hopeful face of the boy whose picture she had sent.

The message following hers was also horribly alarming. Additional threats for legal action in bold capitals, as though adjusting the font would make the situation more dire. I read the letter through carefully before sending it to the trash file. It was basically the same as all the rest had been, the primary difference was they had found someone who could write better English.

Tea brewed, emails read and discarded, I decided to see what I could throw together for dinner. I had nearly forgotten the care package Lily had sent home with me. Eggplant Parmigiana sounded like a good plan. Chaz probably wouldn't be home for another hour, so I had plenty of time to prepare it.

When I cleared the table so I would have room to work, I noticed the same paper Alistair had spread out on his desk, opened to the page with my picture clearly printed on the top left hand corner. I couldn't imagine how it had even made it to the paper. Alistair wasn't that notable in Montreal's film industry, and despite my recent brush with fame, it had merely been a thirty second celebrity dash.

I sat down at the table, tea and eggplant forgotten and began to read the article. It briefly touched on the film Alistair was working on, linked him to his brother, the actor, and finally got around to my part in the whole thing. It was silly, really, labelling me as a gold-digger. First chasing after Adam and then going after Alistair when that didn't pan out for me. It highlighted my stint in the

Money, Masks & Madness

YouTube video, even offering a URL link should anyone wish to take a look. The final blow was my involvement with Chaz at the fashion show.

Basically, this entertainment rag was making me out to look like a free-loading, man-chasing, not-so-high-classed whore. Somehow, someone had figured out who my father was and had even thought to bring his drug-dealing past into it all. It didn't matter to me that he wasn't my biological father. What did matter was that eventually Iris, Daisy, Rose, and Lily would see this paper and be horribly hurt by it. They didn't know their father had an entirely new family and it would undoubtedly devastate them.

Sitting at the table, my tea grew cold as I pondered the situation. I would be surprised if Iris didn't know her father had another family and had been living a free and easy life for the past ten years or more. She had probably kept it from us, thinking she was protecting us, just as I was unwilling to share my knowledge with her. After all, Jean-Pierre Belanger (this was the only way I could think of him now) hadn't seemed the least bit surprised to see me. In fact, looking back, the entire situation looked mildly contrived with the boys going outside to play and him and his wife inviting us in without knowing for sure who we were. Travis had probably told Iris all he knew.

I heard the jiggle of our sticky lock and knew Chaz was about to enter the apartment. He had obviously read the article this morning and left it out for me. With a start, I realized an entire hour had passed already. If we wanted dinner sometime before midnight, I was going to have to come up with plan "B".

"You're home." He sounded strange, like his voice

was balancing between surprise and annoyance.

"Where else would I be?"

"I thought maybe you and Alistair might have another date." The words were casual, but the undercurrent of hurt cut deep into my heart.

"Why would you think that?" This wasn't the conversation I had been expecting. Sure, I had thought there might be some awkwardness between us, but this was bordering on hostile.

He gestured toward the paper, nearly sweeping it onto the floor. I could tell by his exaggerated movements that he'd been drinking. At least, I hoped it was alcohol and not something else. "According to the latest gossip, you two are quite an item."

"Seriously? This entire paper is slanderous. I can barely stand Alistair at the best of times. He's not the sweetest cookie in the jar."

"But he's still a cookie and you've had a taste." Chaz sat across from me and buried his head in his hands. "You should have told me there was something going on between you two. No wonder you were trying to sneak out this morning."

I picked up the paper and proceeded to crumple it into a little ball. Trying for some levity, I tossed it at Chaz's head. It bounced off and rolled onto the floor. He looked up at me with a scowl, but at least I had his attention.

"Listen, there's nothing going on between me and Alistair or his brother or anyone else for that matter. If there was, I wouldn't have slept with you last night or this morning."

"Last night you were afraid of your own shadow; you would have snuggled up to anyone with a beating heart and healthy skin."

I retrieved the paper from the floor and tossed it into the recycle bin. If I knew I wouldn't set off the smoke detector, I would have burnt it. Obviously the man was in a mood. So much for seeking support and advice from the person formally known as my best friend. He'd known me for ages, I couldn't imagine why he would believe the nonsensical lies the reporter had written.

Unfortunately, I had missed the bin when I tossed the scrunched up ball, so I had to pick it up again. This time, a name near the headline caught my attention. Carefully, so I wouldn't tear the now fragile paper, I opened it up and smoothed out the creases. Below the headline was a familiar picture that I had overlooked when I first read the article. Below that portrait the byline read R. Garden. Here I had been worrying about approaching my sisters when this one was out to sell my soul in order to advance her career. *How could she?*

In the process, she had probably ruined my relationship with Chaz. Frustrated, I tore the paper into tiny bits, grabbed my purse and keys from the hook near the door and slammed out of the apartment. Chaz continued to sit there watching me in alarm. At least he had snapped out of his "woe is me" lethargy. I was going to track her down and kill her with my own hands. Well, maybe not kill her, but I was going to do some serious damage.

Jennifer Bogart

Chapter Twenty-four

The repeated pounding on Rose's apartment door had her neighbours peeking their heads out to see what the ruckus was about. I didn't care. I knew she was in there, the television blaring in the background along with a shuffling noise as someone peered through the peephole were obvious giveaways.

"I know you're in there, Rose! Open the damn door!" My fists continued to beat at the door. It was probably a good thing it was cased in steel as I'm sure I would have broken the wood by now. "I can stand out here all night."

Behind me, I heard one person quietly say, "Do you think we should call the police?"

"Isn't that the girl from the paper?" another asked.

I turned to glare at them. "She's my sister. Go ahead and call the police if you want, but you'll miss all the gossip, you nosy old hens." Obviously they had read the paper, checked out the YouTube links, and decided I was the bad guy in this scenario.

"Rose! If you don't answer the door this minute I'm going to call a lawyer and have you charged with libel! Then we'll see how far you get in—" The door swung open, a hand reached out, grabbed my arm, and pulled me inside with a jerk. Behind me, I heard the disgruntled murmur of bystanders followed by the closing of their own doors.

"It's about time," I muttered.

Rose looked awful. She was wearing a ratty old bathrobe, her feet were bare, and her hair was a natty nest of knots. She gestured for me to come in and sit down. I didn't feel much like sitting. Despite how horrible she looked, I still wanted to wring her neck.

"I'm sorry."

"No, you're not."

I took a good look at her and tried to figure out how much of her attire was manufactured. Rose took great pride in her pretty blond appearance. She spent far too much money on expensive salon styles, purchased brand name clothes, and never, ever let the world see her looking anything but her best. Last year when she had had influenza she had still insisted on wearing her satin bathrobe and having her hair slicked back in a becoming style. I couldn't imagine where she had managed to find such an ugly robe until I realized it was one I had left behind before I moved out of her apartment and in with Chaz last year.

"I want to know why?" Actually, I wanted to know a whole hell of a lot more than that, but I figured I had to start somewhere.

Sighing heavily, she sat on the arm of a chair and thought for a long moment. I couldn't begin to imagine what kind of a story she was trying to concoct in her head. "I didn't have much of a choice. Either I wrote the article, or my editor was going to send me packing."

"Right." She had to have had options. Most of what she had written had been badly contrived.

"It's true. Lately your picture has been popping up all over: first with Adam Green at that bar, then on YouTube, and again on Facebook. And don't forget the Saturday paper for that ridiculous fashion show. Snapping a photo of you with Alistair was easy enough to do. It wasn't like I set out to hurt you or anything. If anything, you should be grateful."

"My private life is on display for the world to see, why on earth would I be grateful?" I started pacing the room, unable to sit quietly in her presence. "Do you have *any* idea what you've done with this article? Do Iris, Daisy, and Lily know about this? They'll be devastated when they read about their father!"

"He's your father too!"

I snorted, rolled my eyes and looked away. At least that hadn't been part of the article. Of course, if she found out, she could always run a companion piece which might draw in a few more gossip mongers. "You didn't answer my question."

"Iris must know. Travis gave me Dad's address; I went to see him on Sunday." Rose picked up a magazine and started fanning herself with it.

"Why don't you take that ridiculous robe off? You must be sweltering in it." I didn't want her pathetic performance of self-remorse. "If Iris knew, why didn't she say anything to us?"

Rose shrugged out of the offensive robe, revealing sleek designer slacks coupled with a sleeveless blouse, and did her best to smooth out her frizzed hair. It was going to take a bit more than sweaty palms to get that mop under control. "Probably to protect us. You know how she is, always treating us like stupid little kids. For once I wanted to show off what I could really do."

"Well, you sure showed us, didn't you?" I looked around her tastefully decorated apartment. Even though the furnishings were sparse, each piece was a study in elegance. In contrast, the apartment I shared with Chaz was filled with mismatched bits of this and that. I liked mine better, it was cozier.

"Look, I'm sorry if it bothered you, but it's not like I wrote anything that would ruin your fragile reputation or anything. You work for Alistair Green, he'll be thrilled with the publicity. That fashion show you were in Friday night is already old news, so highlighting it in the paper actually works to the designer's advantage. Fame is fleeting and people will forget about it soon enough."

An image of Chaz sitting hunched over our little kitchen table flitted through my mind. "No, they won't."

I sat back down and closed my eyes. If Rose wrote it, Chaz would believe it. He had no reason not to; the evidence was there in the pictures.

"Come on, Tulip. There isn't anything that bad. It's not like you're in a serious relationship with anyone. Iris, Daisy, and Lily won't care much and our mother isn't likely to pick up the paper and read it. I can't remember the last time she read one of my articles."

"Right." I couldn't tell her about Chaz. At this point, I didn't know if there was anything to tell about him. "Do you know what Alistair thinks about this?"

Rose shrugged her shoulders. "You tell me. You're the one who works for him."

I thought back to this morning, remembering the paper spread out on his desk. He'd left it there like a beacon and I had ignored it. Briefly, I had glanced at the headline, not caring about the byline or the actual story. They had all seen it and not said one word to me.

"Yeah... I guess he'd be happy for the free marketing." Rose was right, Alistair would take the publicity for what it was and I couldn't blame him. His business needed the exposure if he ever wanted to get out of the 'B' horror genre and into something more serious.

"He wasn't angry when he saw it?"

I shook my head. No, of course not, he had been delighted in his own little quirky Alistair way.

"See—no worries." Rose smiled, relief evident on her pretty features.

"Right—no worries. I need to... I have to go."

I needed to get away from her before her apathy started to rub off on me. Rose had always been something of a cat, no matter the kind of scrapes she got into; she always landed on her feet. Since I couldn't bring myself to tell her about Chaz, I had no way of explaining to her how deeply she had offended me by her little stunt. It was one thing to end up in the limelight because of insensitive strangers, quite another because of a greedy goal-oriented sibling.

I walked for about an hour, wandering the streets of Montreal, enjoying the cool evening air as the clouds rolled in, threatening a fierce summer storm. Their grey countenance matched my grim mood. When the sky finally did open up, I welcomed the rain. It hid my tears of frustration and cooled my hot shame-filled cheeks.

This entire situation was why I didn't want to have a romantic relationship with Chaz. As my best friend, he would have supported me, listened to what I had to say and even defended me. As my lover, a seemingly jealous one at that, it wasn't the same. Sex complicates things. We had been walking on this tightrope, balancing precariously between friendship and romance and instead of toppling to one side or the other, the rope had simply snapped in half.

When I arrived home, I was soaked through, but starting to come to terms with all that had happened. I would talk to Chaz, tell him what he had read was a mistake and that we really were better off being friends. He might be my soul mate, but I'd rather live with him as my forever friend than have to deal with all the complications one night of sex had brought into our relationship.

I had expected to find Chaz flipping from one thing to the next or an empty apartment. Instead, I found a room full of people I didn't know. Briefly I wondered if Chaz had thought to throw a little misery party for himself, but dismissed that thought. It wasn't his style to wallow in misery for long. He was more the type to be out partying and making new friends.

"Tulip Garden?" A man in a dark suit approached me, hand extended. Confused, I reached for it, and then remembered my soggy state.

"Yeah—that's me. But I'm wet." His brown eyes took in my drenched clothing and he withdrew his hand, obviously rethinking his greeting.

"We have a few questions for you." Another man stepped forward, also dressed in a suit, but he looked a little less put together, as though he was accustomed to dealing with computers, not people.

"Am I in trouble?" I searched for Chaz, who was sitting on the couch watching us. His lips turned up in a funny little smirk and I wasn't quite sure what to make of his expression.

"We're with a division of the RCMP who investigates fraudulent internet activity. Your IP address has been brought to our attention."

Could this day get any worse? I glanced at Chaz for help, but he shook his head. Obviously they hadn't been willing to speak to him or he was still miffed with me and wasn't about to help me out of this sticky situation.

"Can I take a minute to change?"

I was starting to shiver and water was pooling at my feet on the carpet. The brown-eyed man nodded and gratefully I escaped their prying eyes. I wished Chaz had followed me into my bedroom, but the moment that thought entered my head, I blushed. Actually, considering I needed to strip down to nothing, that wouldn't have been a good idea after all. I wished I could talk to him. He had told me that everything was probably fine as far as the money and Mrs. Akiss were concerned. Quickly I dried off, changed into jeans, and t-shirt and made my way back out to our living room where the two men were still standing where I had left them five minutes earlier.

"Why don't you have a seat?" I motioned to the table where the bits of newspaper from my earlier rant were still scattered. Hastily, I scooped them up. They didn't need to see what had been written on those torn up pages.

Both men assessed the rickety chairs before taking a seat. They were old and tattered, but sturdy enough to hold them.

"I'm Detective Jarvis and this is Sergeant Poirier, we have a few questions for you."

I sat down across from them, feeling horribly outnumbered. "Am I in trouble?" I decided the question needed repeating since they hadn't answered it earlier.

The two of them looked at each other, but it was the dark eyed one, Detective Jarvis, who answered. "That depends on how well you cooperate and your answers, of course."

"Okay." I sat there, listening to the hum of the fridge, the whirr of the fan, and the occasional tsking sound coming from Chaz's direction. Beside my foot was another scrap of the newspaper clipping. Hastily I stomped on it. I had no idea what might have been written on it, but I figured I didn't need any part of that article marring my credibility.

"Have you been in contact with Prince Rashid Al-Haji?"

"No." Well, that was easy enough. Hopefully that was all they needed to know.

Detective Jarvis consulted his list and shot out another, nearly unpronounceable name, to which I answered "no". He continued down his list for nearly fifteen minutes. This was a complete waste of time.

"Mrs. Akiss, claiming to be from Cote d'Ivoire?"

I hesitated, for the tiniest fraction, but I'm sure he saw it. If he hadn't added her location, I might have answered "no" without thinking. Bored as I was with his list of names, I had stopped listening to him after the first ten minutes.

"Mrs. Akiss?" he asked again.

I nodded.

"Now am I in trouble? We emailed each other. I didn't know it was a scam until I received a fake email

Money, Masks & Madness

from PayPal asking me to send money through Western Union to some address in North Africa." I knew I was babbling, but I couldn't help myself. The words tumbled out, tripping over each other in an attempt to escape all at once. "Her letters seemed so sincere and when she sent that picture of her son, my heart broke and I went ahead and sent her the three hundred dollars she needed to start the process of transferring her millions to an offshore account. If I'd had any idea—"

"Shhh… Tulip," Chaz was standing behind me, his hands on my shoulders, forcing me to calm down. After the way he'd acted earlier, his kindness bit deep into my heart. I sank my teeth into my lower lip, trying to quell the trembling.

"You sent her other information too, didn't you?" Sergeant Poirier prompted.

I shook my head, trying to remember the correspondence that had occurred between the two of us. "I sent her the three hundred dollars by PayPal, but that's it. I had refused to give her my banking information. I knew better than that!"

"What about your SIN?"

"Sending someone money isn't a sin." I thought they were from the RCMP, not some kind of religious group.

Jarvis rolled his eyes. "Your Social Insurance Number. Did you send that to her? Along with your picture?"

He held up a printout of the picture I had emailed to her. Since it was obvious he already knew the answer to that one, I wasn't sure why he had bothered to ask the question.

"Sending someone your picture isn't a crime."

"Neither is disclosing your SIN, but it can put you in a pretty awkward position." Sergeant Poirier slid a folder towards me and gestured for me to take a look at its contents.

The file was a complete record of the correspondence between me and Mrs. Akiss. There were other emails in there too, but the ones to her were highlighted. My cell phone record was also there, along with a list of PayPal and banking transactions.

"I don't understand."

"Mrs. Akiss, aka Dr. Sijuwade Bongo, aka Hamza Al-Mustapha and so on tried to steal your identity. You're lucky we caught it in time. A few more weeks and she would have been you."

"But she's in Cote d'Ivoire." Even though Chaz had insisted this was an internet money scam, I couldn't seem to separate the woman I had written to from the cold, calculating thief they were claiming her to be.

"Yes, he probably is. Or possibly in the UK. These guys are pretty adept at faking IP addresses."

"So, I'm not in trouble?" I was trying to sort out all this information, but my brain was starting to shut down on me. The combination of little sleep, a stressful day, and the emotional storm Rose's article had whipped up were starting to take their toll.

"No. You're not really in trouble. You'll need to sign a few papers, close your PayPal and existing bank accounts, and we'll start the process of issuing you a new SIN. For the most part you're a lucky girl."

"How did you know about this? How did you know about me?" All this time I had thought my emails were private.

"CIRA—the Canadian Internet Registration Authority, had received numerous reports regarding specific IP addresses in and around Montreal. This particular group was trying to establish a fraudulent domain in Canada and were collecting social insurance numbers in order to succeed. Yours was one of several that came up as being suspicious in the list."

"Just as simple as that?" I couldn't believe they had accessed all my private information without my ever knowing about it. Didn't they need a warrant or something in order to pull that off?

"Didn't you need a warrant to search Tulip's private files?" Chaz asked as I was thinking the words.

Detective Jarvis shrugged his shoulders in response. "This is surface research; most of it can be easily accessed with a simple phone call to the right person. We weren't investigating you because we thought you were involved. We were investigating you for your protection."

I sighed in relief, but could tell Chaz was actually more upset now than he had been while they were questioning me. "So you march in here, scare her half to death, making her think she got mixed up in some sort of horrible scheme, and now you tell her she wasn't ever in any trouble?"

"Chaz, it's fine." I stood and put a hand on his shoulder, trying to calm him down. "I should have been more careful."

"Yes, you should have." The two officers gathered their papers together and stood up to leave. "You can't go around trusting everyone on the internet."

Or in real life, either, I added silently. "Right. I'll go take care of my banking and PayPal accounts. I guess I should probably change my email and any other internet accounts I have too."

It was going to be a very long night.

Jennifer Bogart

Chapter Twenty-five

Bank accounts frozen with appointments made for the following day to open new ones, PayPal cancelled, Facebook deleted, and new email address set up, it was time to face Chaz and deal with our early evening spat. I learned the hard way I couldn't "let things be" with the hope they would sort themselves out.

"About that article," I said as I sat down beside him on the couch, "Rose pieced bits of this and that together, trying to make an impression on her editor."

"I guess it worked. She nearly got a full page spread."

I smiled wryly. "It was a pretty good story, even though it wasn't true."

Chaz shifted his weight so I could lean on him. He put his arms around me and held me in comfortable silence.

"You know there's nothing going on between Alistair and me." I had to say the words aloud, to ensure we were on the same wavelength. I was done with childish misunderstandings. "There never was. In fact, tomorrow I'm going to give my notice and start looking for a new job."

"You don't have to quit your job because I had a moment of jealousy."

"Don't worry, I'm not. I learned a lot from Alistair and the rest of them and now it's time to move on. I need a grown-up job with more stability." I sighed and turned to look at him. Slowly, I traced my index finger along his temple, following the line of his cheek and coming to rest at the corner of his mouth. His lips quirked in the tiniest smile, which I took as an open invitation. Reaching up I laid a gentle kiss on his mouth, but didn't linger. We still had talking to do.

"I'm sorry about earlier." He tightened his arms around me, as though afraid I was about to pull away from him.

"I know. I'd like to say "it's okay", but it's not. Not really."

"I don't know what I was thinking. I just… "

"Sex changes a relationship. It makes you think you can lay claim to something that doesn't really belong to you."

"When did you get so smart?"

"I'm not. I always felt like that. I watched my mother fade into nothing because a man had convinced her to move away from her family, have babies, and live in seclusion. She was compelled to stay with him even though she had obviously given up on both their relationship and her own needs. I watched her go from being someone who cared to someone who is bitter and angry. I never want to be that person."

"I don't think you have it in you to be like that." Now his fingers were doing the wandering, sliding under my t-shirt, and tickling their way up my spine.

"There's more to it than that."

"I had a feeling." He shifted his weight so I lay comfortably between his thighs, our bodies stretched out on the couch. His fingers continued to dance and tease along my skin, but I knew he was listening to me.

"Before... before we . . ."

I blushed, not quite with embarrassment, but rather a different kind of emotion. "Before last night, things weren't complicated between us. If I needed something, you were there supporting me, not judging and not feeling obligated beyond that of being a good friend. We're not perfect. No one is. At some point, we're going to do horrible things to hurt each other. It might be a simple misunderstanding, it might not even be anyone's fault, but we're going to. When that happens, we won't have the solidity of our friendship to fall back on. Instead, we'll have a gaping hole we created all on our own because our hormones ran amok."

"Do you think you might have this backwards, Buttercup? My parents have been married for thirty years. They fight, ignore each other, and sometimes, yeah, they hurt each other. But no matter what, they're always there for each other. They are best friends. That's what I thought would happen with us. The attraction has always been there between us, it was just a matter of time."

"But this afternoon... you were so angry."

"People get angry and then they cool down, rethink the situation and figure things out. Obviously I didn't stay angry for long." His hands were becoming bolder and I squirmed, shifting my weight so I was lying on top of him.

"You wouldn't have been angry if you'd felt you could trust me."

"I do trust you."

The look I gave him clearly stated my doubt.

"Look, it was a blip in my reasoning. This morning you acted like you were torn between staying with me and bolting. It's not like we discussed any of this, so I wasn't sure if maybe you were feeling guilty. I should know you better than to think you would sleep with me while in a relationship with someone else." He shrugged his shoulders and gave me his model's pout. "B'sides, I was feeling a little insecure. The paper linked you to both Adam and Alistair—most women would be walking on clouds to have that association."

"Hmm… I don't know about that. Besides, I'm not most women." His fingers were beginning to make me feel tingly and hot. I loved the feel of him, his heartbeat constant against me, his breath mingling with mine.

"No, you're not," he murmured before capturing his lips with mine. I guess he figured the conversation was over. I leaned into him, exploring his body, enjoying the sensation of his lips. This was a terrific way to end an absolutely horrible day.

Morning came far too quickly. I would have preferred to stay snuggled up beside Chaz, but I knew I had a ton of work to do. I stretched, rolled out of bed, and glanced back at Chaz who continued to sleep peacefully. It wasn't in my nature to stay in bed too long. No matter how late I went to bed the night before, I woke up early, usually with the first rays of sun.

After a quick shower, I put the kettle on to make tea and sat down at my laptop to check my email. When I realized what I was doing, I chuckled softly and switched off the computer. There wouldn't be any email to check since I had cancelled all my accounts the night before. Even though I had set up a new one, I hadn't take the time to repopulate the address book or send out emails advising anyone of the address change. I was glad Chaz had thought to save all of that information in a separate file so I wouldn't lose them completely. We did, however, make sure we deleted addresses directly related to Mrs. Akiss. It turned out she wasn't emailing me from one account, but from several, to make it more difficult to track her location.

Expecting Chaz to make an appearance any second, I started pulling things out of the fridge to make breakfast. The apartment had cooled down significantly with the rain, so I decided I would treat us both to French toast. We still had a few fresh berries from Lily's that would go with it perfectly.

As I was about to mix the eggs, the doorbell rang. Thinking it might be more to do with my Nigerian adventure, I raced to answer it.

"Are you okay?" It was Iris, in full panic mode. She didn't even wait for me to say hello, much less open the door.

"Of course I'm okay. Why?" I stepped aside, letting her into the apartment.

"Your phone was busy all night and when I tried to email you it kept bouncing back. When I tried to phone you again this morning and got another busy signal, I thought I should come over and see that you were okay for myself."

I rolled my eyes and glanced over to the telephone. Sure enough, the receiver was off the hook. "I'm a grown-up, Iris. Everything is fine. I'm employed, I have a roof over my head and food in my fridge. I can't imagine why you would begin to think something is wrong."

Iris sat herself at the table, making herself at home in my tiny apartment. "You didn't see that horrible article Rose wrote? You know she said all that stuff because her editor was threatening to fire her."

"I saw it. I wasn't impressed."

"She didn't mean any of it. Rose would never do anything to hurt you, at least not on purpose."

I couldn't believe Iris was here in person, at six in the morning, trying to smooth things over between Rose and me. There had to be more to her impromptu visit than this. After all the craziness with the RCMP in my apartment last night, I had pretty much forgotten about Rose's article and all its juicy bits of gossip.

"Rose has her own agenda in life and tends to trample anything that gets in her way. As far as I'm concerned, I'm pretty sure she sees me as an annoying weed, better left plucked and discarded so I can't take root."

"Huh?" Iris sounded confused and I began to wonder if we were talking about the same thing.

"Oh, you know, Rose only notices me when I get in the way. What she wrote about Alistair and Adam is idle gossip. Good for their careers and in the long, no harm done, since apparently no one got hurt."

"Yes, yes of course." She was quiet for a moment longer before asking, "Did you read the part about our father?"

"It was kind of hard to miss." So, she wasn't here because she was worried about the gossip Rose had written about me. Instead, she was concerned about the man who walked out of our lives over fifteen years ago.

"You aren't upset by it?"

"No. I already knew. I went to see him on the weekend." *Had that only been a couple days ago? It felt like a lifetime.* "I guess you already knew too?"

"I wanted to tell all of you the truth, but didn't know how without hurting anyone. Especially Lily. She was the closest to him."

"I wouldn't be surprised if Lily already knew," Chaz announced. He was standing in the doorway of my bedroom, dressed in skimpy boxers. Leisurely, he reached up and stretched, his hands nearly touching the ceiling. When he saw the expression on Iris's face, he grinned. "Good morning, Iris. Stopping in for breakfast?"

"Go put some clothes on," I scolded him, trying not to laugh. The expression on my sister's face was priceless.

"Was he?... What?... Why was he in your room? Did you switch?"

"No, that's my room." At this point I didn't feel I owed Iris an explanation regarding my personal life. She had kept her own secrets. In fact, it was entirely possible she already knew we didn't share a father.

"But... I thought . . ."

I smiled, unable to let Iris wallow in curious discomfort. "Yeah, we're together. It's new, so don't go getting all upset about me not telling you. Besides, it's not like you haven't kept a few secrets yourself."

"Wow, Tulip, I don't know what to say." All of a sudden she looked disappointed.

"There isn't anything to say. Chaz and I have been friends since forever. Not that it's any of your business, but we decided—" I stopped, not sure what we had decided, if anything.

"I can't say I'm surprised. Rose did say something about you getting caught up in the wilder side of Montreal's social life. Latex fashion shows, YouTube videos, affairs with actors… it was only a matter of time for your true nature to emerge."

"I told you all that stuff was lies. Well, not the part about the fashion show, but I was doing someone a favour and needed the cash." Iris was driving me crazy, flipping from one topic to another. This wasn't like her at all. "Are you okay?"

She shook her head, as though to clear away the cobwebs and smiled. "Of course I'm okay."

Right. Of course she was. Just like I'm tough and capable of doing everything for myself.

"I know something is bothering you and it's not me. It's like you're using my personal life to avoid talking about something that's bothering you."

"Mom called me last night. She said you two had a fight."

My mouth dropped open in surprise. "She actually picked up the phone and dialed?"

"Yeah. I guess maybe the guilt got to be too much for her."

Now I was seriously getting worried. In the past week, my entire world had toppled upside down. I knew better than to expect things to slide back into place, some things would be forever off kilter, but I could live with that.

"So you're not here about Rose's article?"

Iris shook her head. "Rose is an idiot, but I don't think she meant any harm in what she wrote."

I sighed heavily, not wanting to deal with the subject of our mother. "Fine. I'll call her again later tonight and smooth things over."

Iris smiled, stood and leaned over to give me a quick hug. Before I could pull away, she whispered in my ear, "Be careful, Tulip. I don't want you getting hurt by this crazy lifestyle of yours."

"I'll be fine." If she had any idea of all the trouble I'd already been in, she would be freaking out. I guess there were some things she was better off not knowing.

Jennifer Bogart

Chapter Twenty-six

Strangely enough, I arrived early to the office, beating Alistair by ten minutes, which almost never happens. A glance at the calendar confirmed the deadline for the masks was quickly approaching. I set to work, sorting Alistair's desk, organizing papers and figuring out his schedule for the day. Considering I was among the last to leave in the evening, the man sure made a giant mess of things in a short amount of time.

Underneath a pile of trade magazines I found a scrap of paper with a phone number scrawled on it. Not knowing whether or not it was important, I simply left it visible on the desk for him to deal with later. The rest was routine tidying. Alistair has issues with picking up after himself. Maybe he's one of those men whose mother did everything for him as a child and he expected to move out, get married, and have his wife take care of him. I can't even begin to imagine what his house looks like.

Next, I tackled setting up the new coffee machine. It arrived late the day before, but there hadn't been time to take it out of the box. It was easily half the size of the original one, leaving counter space for mugs and other coffee paraphernalia. At first glance, this one looked easier to manage, but the closer I looked at it, the more gadgets and gizmos I found on it. Why couldn't he have purchased a Keurig or Tassimo or any other one-cup wonder that was on the market?

"Good morning, Tulip," Paige said as she sauntered into the office. She looked at the machine I was running water and vinegar through and shook her head. I didn't know if her look of disgust was for me or the coffee maker, but I didn't bother to say anything.

Dieter and Derek were close behind Paige and I wondered if maybe the three of them had some kind of creative meeting this morning. Usually they were all here, working away at their masks long before I made an appearance. Alistair was still nowhere to be seen. For some reason, that made me uneasy.

Neither of them took note of me and my french-fry smell as they passed through the kitchen area and headed to their work stations. I could see them setting up from where I stood at the machine and wondered what was going on this morning. Normally, Dieter at least had something friendly to say. Finished with the cleaning, I decided to put the new toy to the test by brewing a cup. Thankfully it gurgled to life, filling the office with the aromatic smells of freshly brewed coffee.

"You're early, Petal," Alistair said from behind me. I hadn't heard him come in over the sounds of the coffee maker. "I see you got that up and running. Good."

I smiled absently at him and sighed in resignation. Obviously, he was never going to change his ways. With all that had happened in the past twelve hours, I felt like a stranger in my own skin. "The first cup is nearly ready, if you want to try it."

Alistair shook his head, confusing me. "I thought I told you yesterday, I'm done with coffee."

Money, Masks & Madness

"What?"

He shrugged his shoulders and curled his lips into a grimace-like smile. "This movie is making me far too jittery, so I've decided to take a break from the coffee thing."

Was he insane? I had a feeling that Alistair's withdrawal from coffee would be worse than watching an alcoholic dry up. Caffeine jitters had to be preferable to addiction angst.

"Okay," I said, annoyance evident in my voice. I wish he had said something before I had wasted my time setting up the machine and cleaning it.

"Perhaps Paige would enjoy a cup?"

Paige was the last person I was going to make coffee for. "Actually, I think I'll have this one. The directions are here, I'm pretty sure Paige is capable of brewing her own coffee."

Forgetting the fact that I don't even drink coffee, nor do I put sugar in anything, I poured two heaping teaspoons of the white stuff into it and took a sip of the steaming brew. Trying not to grimace at the bittersweet taste, I followed Alistair to his office, ready to take orders for the day. As he started listing his mundane tasks, my mind wandered out of the room and into a world that was fresh and new. I needed to find another job, but I couldn't imagine what I would be able to do with my limited skills and work experience.

The weekend couldn't arrive soon enough. Each day I went to work, determined to give Alistair my resignation, but unable to quit without having some kind of income. Chaz had assured me numerous times that he could cover the rent for the two of us, but I wasn't about to take our relationship there. It was strange enough we had fallen into a pattern of romance in place of our easy friendship. Relying on him financially didn't seem like a good plan. I trusted him, and if I were honest, I could even admit to loving him. How could I not? I felt like I'd known him forever and not for the few years I had lived in Montreal.

My mind returned to the present and I remembered I was supposed to be getting ready to take the train out to my mother's house. My original plan had been to ask Chaz for a ride, but I had thought better of it. I needed to have this face-to-face conversation with her alone. From the day I met him, Chaz had been my champion; I think it was time I started championing myself.

My mother's house was the same as I remembered: small and convenient. Since there were three bedrooms, we had all had to share. Iris and Daisy had the medium room, while Rose, Lily and I used what was meant to be the master bedroom. Our mother had used the smallest room until one by one we started to move out.

The summer heat wasn't kind to her gardens. The few surviving plants were withered, browning at the edges, and struggling to stay alive. The lawn was patchy, more populated with dandelions than grass. Even the single tree gracing the front yard had lost half its leaves to a fungus of some sort.

I knocked on the front door, taking note of the peeling paint and sloping front step. The place needed work but I doubted she was up to the task. When my knock brought no response, I rang the bell. Perhaps she hadn't heard me over the buzz of the television. She knew I was coming; I had called the night before to give her fair warning.

Minutes passed and I wondered if perhaps she was avoiding me. Her car was in the driveway, so she couldn't be far. She wasn't one to walk if there was handy transportation nearby. Growing impatient, I rang the bell again. I had a key, but hadn't used it since moving out. I knew I wouldn't want her letting herself into my home uninvited.

The door swung open and I was faced with the angry face of my mother. Pale blue eyes and blond hair, she looked the same as I remembered, except she was a little more faded, as though she had been bleached white by the sun instead of tanning golden brown.

"Well don't stand there letting my air-conditioning escape, come in."

She stepped aside, allowing me to pass. A faint odour of cooked eggs wafted towards me and I stole a glance at the kitchen. Dirty dishes were piled high beside the sink with food leftovers crusted onto them. Part of me wanted to believe it wasn't my problem, but I knew, as her daughter, someone should step in. Our mother was lazy, not neglectful. Something wasn't right here.

"Hello, Mom," I said, as I slid out of my flip-flops. I would have preferred to leave them on my feet after seeing the grimy condition of her floor, but I knew she would be upset if I did, she had raised me better than that. I leaned over to kiss her lightly on the cheek, ignoring her scowl at my warm greeting.

"The cleaning lady has been on holiday, so you'll have to ignore the mess," she called back to me as I followed her down the narrow hall to the living room. "I was putting the kettle on when you arrived. Do you want tea?"

"Sure, tea would be great." I hoped it would be served in a clean cup.

Pleasantries dispatched and weak tea cooling in my cup, I knew the time had come to ask my questions as I sat on the couch from my childhood and tried to ignore the constant noise of the television in the background. As much as I wanted to turn it off, I knew doing so would cause an unnecessary kerfuffle which would result in my never getting any answers.

"I want to talk about my father." The words tumbled out, unrehearsed. I had decided the direct approach would be best.

"There's nothing to tell you that you don't already know. He's a two-time drug dealer who abandoned us ages ago." She took a long sip of her tea, dismissing the conversation.

"He's not my father."

"He's the only father you ever knew."

I sighed, forcing all my frustration to escape my body with that one breath.

"Mom, I hate all this animosity between us. I don't care that you cheated on your cheating husband—"

"He was never my husband."

"Right." I took another deep breath and started again. "I want to know what happened. I have bits and pieces of the story, from Jean-Pierre Belanger, Rose, Iris, and you, but I'd like to be able to put the entire thing together."

Money, Masks & Madness

She got that far off look on her face, the one that told me she was no longer listening. The television continued to broadcast its constant drone, letting me know it was time for yet another game show with loud music and strange sound effects. I began to realize I couldn't force her to tell me anything. Perhaps it was time to give up on the past and live for the future.

And then, she began to talk.

Jennifer Bogart

Chapter Twenty-seven

"Your father came to rescue me."

That was a strange way to start a story, but I decided it wasn't in my best interest to interrupt her at this point.

"I knew him from my childhood. He had warned me about getting involved with Jack, but I had refused to listen, thinking he was jealous of my relationship. We'd had a pact of sorts. If neither of us was married by the time we were thirty, we'd marry each other. He'd be a house husband, stay home and raise the kids while I went to work every day. I always thought it was a joke between us, but a small part of him had been serious.

"He would stop in and visit us, bringing small gifts—books, toys for the girls, and candy. At first, he was careful to come when Jack was home. They had also been friends in high school. Well, they had sort of been friends—as friendly as a best friend and boyfriend could be."

She paused; her lips twitched until a soft smile appeared on her face, making her look younger, softer. Her expression made me think of the way I feel about Chaz and in that moment, I knew she had loved my biological father.

She shook her head, regained focus and started talking again. "His name was Duncan O'Shea. He had the most beautiful red hair, curly and always in need of a good haircut. I used to sit behind him in school, counting his freckles, not that he had many, but I couldn't help myself."

That smile was back, transforming her from the withered old woman she had let herself become to the young girl she had once been. I liked seeing this softer side of my mother, a shimmer of memory beckoned to me, but didn't take shape.

"His visits became more frequent the more Jack was away. I knew about Jack's other family; it seemed so much easier to ignore the signs than to confront him. Duncan made our lives easier, continuing to bring the supplies Jack forgot, keeping me company during his long, lonely absences."

"Did you know about Jack getting arrested?" I was loath to interrupt her fond memories, but I was worried she would stray from the topic.

She nodded, looking me straight in the eye for the first time in years. "Duncan told me shortly after it happened."

"If you knew, why didn't we leave right away? Why did we wait for so long?"

I didn't expect the self-deprecating smile filled with bitterness that crossed her features. Anger, frustration, even sadness I could have handled, but this look of self-hatred unsettled me.

"I hoped Jack would come back to us, forget about that other family and live as we had planned before he got involved in the grow-op."

"What?"

She shrugged her shoulders and shook her head in bewilderment. "We made promises to each other. I did my best to keep up my end of the bargain—except when it came to Duncan. You were the result of one moment of weakness. If it weren't for that red hair of yours . . ."

It was my turn to shake my head. "Even if I had been blond like my sisters, Jack would have known. He can count. Plus, he told me he has a son the same age as me."

"I know. I met him, once."

Could things get any more confusing?

She laughed, shook her head and continued her story. "After you were born, I dedicated my time to creating the world your fa—Jack—and I had set out to. Food came from the land, clothes were homemade, you girls were homeschooled... Life was difficult—harsh at times, but I struggled through, hoping my commitment would lure him back."

I waited, knowing what was coming, but still needing to hear the words.

"It didn't." Tears started to roll down her cheeks and she brushed them away. I've never seen my mother cry.

"I blamed myself, and you—not because I didn't love you, but because you were a constant reminder that my relationship with Jack was an illusion." Her tears started to fall in earnest. Part of me wanted to reach for her, offer her comfort, but I was afraid she'd push me away, given my role in her unhappiness.

"Why did you wait so long for Jack to come back?" I had to ask the question.

"I didn't, not on purpose. At first, I didn't know where he was, but Duncan came to tell me what had happened. It was the first time I saw him since—well—since before you were born. Until then, he didn't even know you existed. I thought I could wait out the nine months for Jack to return. When he didn't return after the original sentence, I assumed he had done something else to have his punishment extended. I didn't realize he'd listed that other family when it came time to do his house arrest. In fact, I didn't even know about the house arrest."

Another long pause, more tears and her eyes faded to some far-off memory I didn't expect her to share. I waited, ignoring the big winnings on the game show, the cheers of the crowd, and the electronic sounds of success. I was beginning to understand my mother's obsession with game shows. They were made of real people, with real emotions, but happy in a synthetic not really important kind of way.

"Duncan told me he'd keep us safe until Jack returned. He promised . . ." Her voice faltered while her eyes filled with tears.

"Mom, what did he promise?" I was trying to be compassionate, but at the same time I was losing patience. "Mom?"

"He promised he would take care of us until Jack was released. I believed him." With shaking hands she reached for a tissue. The announcer's voice on the television was grating at my nerves so I got up, wandered across the family room and switched it off, giving her time to compose herself.

The silence in her little house was broken by sniffles as my mother wiped away the tears she'd been storing for years.

"What happened?" I had a feeling Duncan O'Shea hadn't abandoned her quite the way Jack had.

"He stopped bringing supplies. He just... stopped. We had a routine. He would come once a week with milk, eggs, flour—whatever we needed. The first week he didn't come I wasn't concerned, I thought maybe he was busy or had been distracted. When the second week went by I was annoyed, but by the third week I was torn between being angry and worried. Duncan wasn't like Jack—he wouldn't desert us like that, but I couldn't help thinking..." her voice trailed off in a wave of regret and sadness.

Before her tears could overwhelm her, I asked, "What happened to Duncan?"

Her pale blue eyes met mine and the grief reflected in them filled my heart with despair. "There was an accident... on his way to our cabin. A drunk driver slammed into his truck, forcing it off the road and into a tree."

The image she painted shocked me. I didn't expect her lover to create this kind of emotion in me; after all, I didn't even remember the man. "So he hadn't deserted you."

"Yes, he did," she argued. "He died and left me here alone, not knowing what had happened for years."

I knelt in front of her, grimacing at the grimy carpet as my bare knees made contact. I should have had enough sense to wear capris this morning instead of short shorts. "It wasn't his fault."

"I waited for him, Tulip."

"I know, Mom." I reached up and stroked her cheek, feeling her hot tears on my fingertips. She looked so fragile and I had the strangest feeling it was my fault. "You did your best."

Vehemently she shook her head. "If it weren't for you, he might still be alive."

"What?" This was madness.

"He kept coming back to check on you, to make sure you were safe." Bitterness seeped back into her voice. "If it weren't for you, he wouldn't have been on that road in the first place."

"You don't know that."

"Oh, Tulip. I do. We made a mistake. I was lonely, he was available and things got out of control. It's not much different than you and your hermaphrodite friend." She paused, as though expecting me to object to her description of Chaz, but I chose to ignore her. "I thought I loved him, but it was fleeting. Jack was the love of my life. So you see, if you didn't exist with all that red hair, Duncan would still be alive and Jack wouldn't have found an excuse to live with his other family."

I was beginning to think my mother belonged in a mental institute. "You can't be serious? It's not like I planned to ruin your perfect little fairy tale life. Which, from the sounds of things, wasn't all you had expected it to be."

She shook her head and I could see she was trying to get her thoughts back in order. When I looked at her, all I could picture was Rose with her lies echoing through my head, justifying her actions in an attempt to make herself feel better about them.

I stood and backed away from her. "I think he loved you and all this time you've blamed me so you wouldn't have to feel guilty. Maybe he felt a little guilt over leaving you with another mouth to feed, but he didn't even know I existed until I was nearly seven years old, and even then you probably didn't ask him for help. The thing is you don't have to feel guilty anyway. He was a free man who made his own choices. The only person to blame for his death is the drunk who hit him!"

Money, Masks & Madness

"Tulip—"

"I'm tired of being everybody's scapegoat. You, Alistair, Rose, Mrs. Akiss… I don't need this in my life." I slid my feet into my flip-flops, grabbed my bag and turned to leave. As my hand reached for the doorknob a thousand childhood dreams splintered apart, leaving me with a stark reality in place of the dream I had always believed.

"Maybe you didn't know any better or maybe you and Jack were stupid, but my life wasn't quite the fairy tale Iris has always led me to believe. You neglected me and left my care to her and Daisy. You allowed Rose to torment me even if you didn't encourage it. I don't care anymore if you sit here wallowing in the misery you've created. All this time I thought I was a disappointment to you compared to the rest, when in reality, you didn't care."

My mother stood and came to the door, placing a hand on my arm, she said quietly, "Of all my flowers, you are the hardiest."

"What's that supposed to mean?"

A smile drifted across her face, softening her features. "It means I know I never really have to worry about you. Whatever harsh conditions life throws at you, you manage to overcome them. You persevere, adapt, and change to suit your environment. The rest… they're more fragile."

"I think you have it backwards. They're always checking up on me, making sure I'm doing things the right way, keeping a job, hanging out with good people, staying out of trouble." I snorted, knowing the sound was derogatory, but unable to stop the reaction. "It's like everyone thinks I can't take care of myself—"

"When that's what you've been doing all along," she finished the sentence for me. "Please don't go, Tulip. Stay for dinner so I can get to know you all over again."

I wasn't sure if she was being honest or looking for another way to make her feel better about herself. My inner child still yearned for her attention and approval, while the teenager in me wanted to push her away. It was the emerging adult inside who had the final say.

"I don't think there's much about me you don't already know," I said. "But I'll stay so we can talk; there's still so much about our lives I'd like to know."

She nodded and dropped her hand from my arm. "Should I cook? Or would you rather we order in?"

I glanced nervously at the condition of her kitchen. "Why don't we go out? My treat."

"I... uh..."

Looking at her tattered appearance, I guessed it had been a while since she had left the house. She had no real need, since both grocery stores and pharmacies delivered. "Go take a quick a shower and get cleaned up. I'll wait, I'm not going anywhere."

She nodded, smiled quietly, and turned to go up the stairs.

Chapter Twenty-eight

Having to recreate myself from scratch, in a legal sense, was equivalent to having ice water thrown in my face. It made me realize I had been meandering along in my life, letting things happen to me without taking control and responsibility. After reconnecting with my mother, next on my list of priorities was dealing with my overbearing sisters. I couldn't leave things between Rose and me as they were and I couldn't have Iris continuing to shelter me from the big bad world. I was done with being the little sister, both victim and damsel in distress. This flower was ready to blossom.

Besides, if they didn't already know the entire story, I figured it was time they did. Not sharing a biological father shouldn't have any impact on our relationship, but with my sisters, you never could tell. I also figured it was a good time to tell them about Chaz, unless Iris had already beaten me to it.

Since my apartment was so small, and Chaz's appearances were unpredictable, I decided we should meet at our favourite breakfast restaurant. Small and reasonably priced, I had told them all to meet me there at eight on Sunday morning. Being the chicken I am I had sent the invitation by email instead of calling each of them. The email served two purposes; it let them know I had a new account and kept me from having to endure their endless questions.

"What's with all the secrecy?" Lily asked. She had taken the train in the night before, the same one I had been on coming home from visiting our mother. Fortunately for me, she had spent the night at Iris's since her place was bigger. Even though Lily had plied me with questions, I had kept my resolve to speak to them all at once. I wasn't in the mood to repeat myself.

For once, I was the last to arrive at the restaurant, probably because I spent the past thirty minutes torn between staying snuggled up beside Chaz or braving my sisters and their unending concern.

"Why don't we order and while we eat I'll tell you." I took my seat, flipped open the menu and pretended to study the selection of fancy brunch choices.

"You're not pregnant are you?"

"Rose!" Lily threw a cloth napkin at her, it landed in my glass splattering water everywhere.

I picked it up, wrung it out and placed it on the table, all the while shaking my head and biting back a smile. Trust Rose to ask the most outrageous question.

"I'm only voicing what everyone else is thinking." Rose's mouth turned downwards in a petal-pink pout Marilyn Munroe would have been proud of.

"I'm not pregnant, I'm still employed, and I don't have some not-so-rare sexually transmitted disease."

Money, Masks & Madness

"Just tell us, Tulip." The look of concern on Daisy's face seemed genuine. "Whatever it is, we'll do our best to help you work through it."

"Why do you guys always assume the worst from me? There's nothing *wrong*. For all you know, this is the happiest day of my life."

"Did Alistair propose?" Rose's eyes were two glowing orbs of blue on her otherwise pale face. She looked so tired, making her skin pale even though we were already halfway through summer.

"If he had, there would be a huge ring on her finger," Iris retorted.

"You're all a bunch of children, you know that?" Their nonsense was starting to make me dizzy. "I just… well, I wanted to see all of you. It's been a few weeks since we were all together."

Four pairs of cornflower blue eyes met mine. If disbelief were a palpable thing, we'd all be suffocating right about now.

"Right," Lily muttered. "I didn't desert my farm at the height of my busy season because you were missing me, so spit it out already."

"Fine. Let's start with the good news. Chaz and I are in a relationship. A real one." I expected my announcement to come as a surprise to them since I had spent the last couple of years denying there was anything more than friendship between us. Their responses were varied, but none of them seemed surprised.

"That's it?" Daisy asked. She gave Iris a knowing look, shaking her head and smirking. "Well, okay then."

"Did you tell them already, Iris?"

Iris shook her head in denial. "No, it wasn't my place to share. We aren't surprised, Sweetie, because we all saw it coming."

"I didn't." Rose waved her hand in a gesture of dismissal. "I can't imagine why you'd be interested in him when there are better choices available."

"You mean wealthier choices, right?" Rose's attitude wasn't going to take away from my happiness with Chaz.

She shrugged her shoulders and pretended to study her menu. "Whatever floats your boat, mon amour."

"I think it's lovely," Lily said. "But I don't know why you wanted us all together for this. Iris is right, I'm pretty sure we all saw it coming."

"That's not the real reason I wanted us to get together." I took a sip of water, wishing it were something stronger. This part wasn't going to be easy.

"Well?" Rose's voice was laced with impatience.

I took another slow drink of water, noting the slight chlorinated taste of it. I missed well water. I'd rather have the taste of dirt than added chemicals.

"If it's about your father, we already know," Iris said into the silence.

The water in my mouth shot across the table as I struggled for breath. How could they know?

"We've always known." Daisy patted my hand in a maternal gesture. "Well, maybe not always, but since you were about six or seven. Mom didn't say anything, but it was obvious the red-headed man was your father. He was nice to all of us, bringing us candies and toys. I wonder what happened to him?"

"He died."

We all turned to look at Rose.

Money, Masks & Madness

"Well, he did. Duncan O'Shea was hit by a drunk driver; his truck ended up wrapped around a tree. At the time, airbags weren't common and he wasn't wearing a seatbelt. It's all very cliché." She shrugged her shoulders, nonchalantly dismissing the entire conversation.

We continued to stare at her. The others were probably curious about how she knew so much. Her knowledge didn't surprise me. Rose is a journalist; her job is to know stuff. What I couldn't understand is how long she'd known and why hadn't she said something before now? She was so heartless about it.

"You all knew and didn't tell me?" I thought we shared everything. We were as close as sisters could be. Of course, they were my half-sisters, so maybe that had something to do with it.

"We didn't plan—"

"It's not like—"

"Tulip—"

Lily, Daisy and Iris were tripping over themselves, trying to offer me some kind of explanation for their betrayal. Rose sat back, keeping her silence and waiting for the rest to calm down.

"For Pete's sake, give it a rest," Rose commanded when the noise level at the table began to rise. "They didn't tell you because they were so protective of you, their ragged little weed. I couldn't be bothered—I didn't really care where you came from."

"Rose!" Iris admonished. "You don't mean that."

"Yes, I do. All our troubles started with the arrival of Tulip. Our father hated to be around us; knowing she wasn't his, he took bigger risks, and eventually got caught. Life in our little forest sanctuary wasn't quite what he had expected, so he found comfort somewhere else, *with someone else*. If it weren't for her who knows what kind of life we'd all be living now?"

"I don't think you can blame Tulip for our father's mistakes. From what I understand, he already had another family before Tulip was even born." Iris's logic was lost on Rose.

"Actually—you probably would have had a worse time of it." My voice was quiet, but assured. I hadn't planned to tell them this part of what our mother had revealed to me during our dinner, but I was tired of always being blamed for something over which I had no control.

"Right." Rose leaned back in her chair with her arms crossed over her chest. "This, I've got to hear."

"Not only did my biological father make sure we didn't starve to death after your father disappeared, but when Duncan O'Shea discovered he had a child, he changed his will, to make sure his estate would go to her—me. It wasn't a lot, but it was enough to keep you all clothed, fed and comfortable. Didn't you ever wonder how our mother managed to buy a house and all those appliances on her tiny paycheck? She worked as a cashier in a local clothing store. Duncan left everything to me in trust; mom had control over the estate until I turned twenty-one."

Lily's face creased into a small smile. "I knew it. No wonder she was so protective of you."

"I don't understand."

"Mom was always saying don't let Tulip get hurt, you have to watch out for her, keep her out of trouble, blah, blah, blah. It might not have felt like it to you, but it was like you were her favourite, except she didn't want you to know."

Money, Masks & Madness

"Ha." Rose was still pouting in the corner. "So now what? Are you rich or something?"

I shook my head. "No. I told mom to keep what's left of the money, believe me, there's not much. She needs it more than I do."

Lily, Daisy, and Iris nodded their approval while Rose continued to grumble. I couldn't figure out what her problem was. Obviously she was doing all right with her work as a journalist. I had articles to prove it.

"I can't believe our father has another family." Daisy suddenly announced, her voice was filled with a hurt she couldn't disguise. "Was it easier for him to forget about us and move on?"

Lily shook her head and pursed her lips in thought. "I think maybe it was. Both our parents made so many mistakes—they were young and secluded from the real world. I hate to say it, but maybe his leaving was for the best."

"I'll never forgive him for all that he put us through."

"Rose, no one is expecting you to forgive him for anything." Deep sadness laced Iris's voice. "He is a selfish man. It's stupid that we even care about what he did at this point in our lives."

"Which is why you kept the truth from us all this time," I stated. Finally, things were starting to make sense where my mixed-up family was concerned. "He's not worth our time and energy."

"True," Lily agreed. "I don't think I'll ever be able to forgive him."

"I'm pretty sure he's not all that thrilled to have us around either." Daisy sighed, took a sip of her coffee and turned her attention to something outside of the window.

"Where do we go from here?" Iris asked. She had the strangest look on her face, almost as though she expected things to be different between us.

"Now we order breakfast, gossip about whatever, and carry on as usual. Except, no more secrets." I laughed. "Secrets get you into trouble."

"Right." Rose sat up, leaned forward and released her hold on her pout. "Does this mean we're not holding grudges and we're starting over?"

I shook my head, trying to ease her concerns. "Oh Rose, you're a pain in the ass, but I doubt anyone could stay angry with you for too long."

The others laughed at that, relief washing over them. Things were changing, I was no longer their faltering flower to be protected and shielded, but we'd be okay—somehow, we always were.

"You're on a roll." Chaz was sitting on the couch, flipping through channel after channel of nothing on the television.

"What do you mean?" I had returned from breakfast with my sisters feeling hopeful. Things might never be quite what they were between us, but at least there weren't any more secrets.

"You spent Saturday with your mom and this morning with your sisters. Were you planning another visit to your father this afternoon?" He hit the power button on the remote and the television magically fell silent.

I shook my head and offered him a sad smile. The time had come to fill Chaz in on all the details of my life.

Money, Masks & Madness

"My real dad is dead, it happened years ago. My sisters now know I'm a "love child" for lack of a better word and my mother doesn't hate me, she had issues she needed to work through."

"Right." He stood and stretched, his shirt riding up to show off his washboard abs.

I sighed, lost in the vision for a few seconds. When I realized what I was doing, I blushed and turned away. For years I had admired Chaz in secret, I wondered how long the instinct to hide my attraction to him would last.

"There's still one thing left for me to do while I'm cleaning up my life." I walked towards him, giving him what I hoped was my best "come-hither" smile. I had a feeling I was failing badly, but Chaz didn't care.

He pulled me into his arms and I welcomed the strength in his embrace. "What would that be? Quit your awful job?"

I shook my head, inhaling the unique scent of him. "Nope."

He pulled back to look down at me, the question burning bright in his blue eyes. "No?"

"No. I can't quit yet. I've already drafted my letter of resignation. I'm giving Alistair until Thanksgiving. The shooting will be done by then."

"I don't understand."

"My first thought was to march in there and be done with The Macabre Mercantile once and for all—but I realized that wasn't the best plan. First of all, I owe it to myself to see this job through to the end. It's a stupid movie and I hate the job, but for once in my life I don't want to be giving up on something."

I stepped away, softening the action with a soft smile. Chaz is more sensitive than I had first thought, I didn't want him to get the wrong idea when I left his embrace. "Second, I need the money."

"I told you not to worry about that—"

"For my entire life, I have relied on other people to take care of me. I let my sisters be controlling and overbearing. Unlike most people, I grew up with five mother-hens. I need to start taking responsibility for myself, pay attention to what I'm doing and maybe I'll be able to figure out where I'm going."

Chaz looked down at his hands and I noticed he had painted his nails green. Bizarre, but I didn't expect anything less from him.

"Am I part of where you're going?" His voice was quiet, uncertainty laced through each word he spoke.

"I'm expecting you to be my travel partner." I moved to sit on the couch, hoping Chaz would follow me. Looking up at him all the time gives me a kink in my neck. If I was to tell him, no doubt it would come out sounding like he's a pain in my neck, which I'm sure wouldn't go over so well.

As expected, he settled his weight back onto the couch, placing a hand on my leg and making slow circles with his index finger on my thigh. "I was worried for a minute... I thought maybe . . ."

"Maybe since I've been cleaning house I might toss you out with the dirty dish water?" I shook my head and scooted closer to him. "You're my best friend, my knight in satin armour, my soul mate. I need you in my life. Always have, always will. Of all the madness I've been dealing with, you've been my one constant. I could never let you go."

Money, Masks & Madness

I reached up, placed my hands on either side of his face and pulled him closer for a kiss. Before my eyes drifted shut I caught the shadowy hint of eyeliner and mascara that soap and water hadn't been able to wash away. As our lips met, I couldn't resist a playful nip at him. Only Chaz would spend the morning experimenting with make-up while fretting about the state of our relationship.

Jennifer Bogart

Epilogue

Once upon a time, when the world offered adventure, the sun twinkled hope and the birds chirped excitement, Tulip discovered the secret of the universe. It didn't sparkle with mystical powers nor was it contrived of wondrous words. It was pure simplicity.

Around her, the forest whispered words of wisdom, sending them through the leaves on a gentle breeze. The cabin, nestled deep within nature's beauty, showed signs of disrepair and neglect, but Tulip knew there was more to it than its tattered visage. Love flourished here; she could feel its essence in everything the sun touched.

"Are you sure this is the place?" Prince Charming stood at her side, splendid in yellow satin with the backdrop of autumn behind him.

Tulip nodded. "Yes. Perfect, isn't it?"

Chaz surveyed the area, being careful to keep his thoughts to himself. It needed work. No electricity, no running water, and no convenient take-out restaurants nearby. This might kill him. "Uh... it's a bit rustic."

"Come on, Chaz, you agreed to this." Tulip took his hand and led him toward the cabin. Despite its weathered appearance, it was a sturdy shelter, the shuttered windows and barred door had kept the forest critters at bay. Either that or someone had made periodic visits to ensure it didn't fall completely into ruin.

"That was before I realized we'd be living on the set of "Anne of Green Gables"," he grumbled. "I don't think I'm dressed for this."

Tulip's laugh echoed through the forest, startling birds into flight. "I packed jeans and sweatshirts for you. You'll be fine."

"Tell me why we're doing this again?" When he smiled, the world tilted, gave a little shudder, and settled back into place, exactly as it should be.

"Because this is where it all started, silly." Tulip slipped the key into the lock and smiled when she heard the click as the mechanism released. "It's going to be fun."

"I bet it's dirty in there." Chaz shuddered. "I'm not a fan of getting dirty."

"What's a little dirt between friends?"

He responded with a raised eyebrow while wrapping his arms around her. Standing as she was, with the sun filtering through her fiery red hair, Tulip was the most beautiful person he had ever met: inside and out.

A quick glance around told Tulip the cabin was as spotless as it had been left fifteen years earlier. Her sisters had been busy.

"I think there might be spiders lurking in the corners." Chaz shuddered, tightening his arms around her. "I'm going to need protection."

"This is a magical place, free of Chaz-eating spiders. The fairy godsisters came by earlier to sweep away the dust. If we're lucky, we might even find food in the refrigerator, compliments of Lily. When we finished filming the segments of "Dread the Dead" at her farm, she was eager to get back to regular work."

Money, Masks & Madness

"Why would you have a refrigerator when there's no hydro?"

"Can't you hear the hum of the generator? We have every modern convenience at our fingertips except for television, telephones, and internet. But I think we'll be able to find something to occupy ourselves."

Tulip stepped out of his reach and spun around in the spacious living room. The cabin wasn't exactly as she had remembered it. The couch and chairs had been replaced, the dishes on the shelves were new and someone had thoughtfully placed out-of-season tulips in a vase in the middle of the dining table. It was the perfect place to spend quality time with her new fiancé.

She stopped suddenly, taking a moment to let the world stop spinning. "I can't believe we're doing this."

"What?"

"Leaving the city behind." A look of wonder crept into her warm brown eyes.

"It's only for a week—don't get carried away and start thinking we're staying here forever. You're starting a new job with that marketing firm." Chaz's gaze swept over the windows and darted nervously towards the door. "You know, this is the kind of place where zombies attack."

"I'll keep you safe," she insisted, stepping towards him. "I'm practically a certified zombie expert, you know."

Reaching up on tiptoes, Tulip trailed gentle kisses along Chaz's jaw until she reached his lips. Her tongue darted out, tasting and teasing playfully. Resting her hands on his chest, she gave a gentle push, preventing him from pulling her fully into his embrace.

"Come on, I want to show you something."

Tulip took his hand and led him back outside. Not bothering to lock the door behind her, she pulled her prince deep into the shadowy forest. The further they walked, the quieter it became, with only a light breeze rustling crisp leaves to break the silence. As she had while spinning in the cabin, Tulip stopped suddenly, inhaled deeply, and looked at Chaz earnestly.

"This is paradise. You, me, and Mother Nature. No money, no masks, and no madness."

Chaz smiled at her, mischief dancing in his eyes. In that moment, he knew Tulip was right; this is all they would ever need.

And they lived happily ever after...

About the Author

Reader, writer, editor, explorer, dreamer… Jennifer Bogart is having a love affair with words.

Currently the author of three women's fiction novels (Newvember and Hot Dogs are Diet Food), two romantic short stories (Under the Stars and Seven Seconds), and a YA fantasy series (Liminal Lights and Shadow Shifts published by Morning Rain Publishing), she can't stop writing any more than she can stop breathing. You can follow Jennifer on Facebook, Twitter, Instagram, and her blog.

http://www.jenniferbogart.com/
https://www.facebook.com/JenniferBogartAuthor
jenny-b@live.ca

CPSIA information can be obtained
at www.ICGtesting.com
Printed in the USA
LVOW10s1939220418
574426LV00005B/26/P